# WINNING THE GALLOWS FIELD

*A Tale of Bladesend*

# WINNING the GALLOWS FIELD

*A Tale of Bladesend*

# Elaine Isaak

Winning The Gallows Field
appeared on ElysianFiction.com, Summer 2001

© 2001, Elaine Isaak

Formatted by: emtippettsbookdesigns.com

# CHAPTER
# ONE

### *Homecoming*

PANTING, TRELAYNE CLASPED HIS SWORD in both hands and drove toward the shifting scales of the dragon's neck as it reared its huge head through the hole in the ceiling. Flinging aside Loref's shredded body, the dragon lunged to meet him, its crimson nostrils flaming. As they met, Trelayne's wounded knee gave out beneath him, twisting him sideways and down, away from the dragon's fire. The sword buried itself in dragon's flesh, acid blood streaming forth to burn his hands.

A great gout of flame trumpeted with the dragon's last breath, searing past Trelayne's face toward the lofty ceiling. Already the fine carvings of the feast hall smoked and caught. Trelayne lay with gritted teeth as the acid burned his hands, he rolled on his side, body clenched. Through his blood-matted hair, he forced himself to look to the sorceress Kilsharne.

An unearthly howl rose from the table where she stood. A new and magical agony ripped through Trelayne, and he screamed.

Kilsharne's silk sleeves flew as her hands cut the shape of magic from the air. At her feet, his retainer, Derik, lay trapped by the bulk of a huge barrel. His eyes reflected his terror, but, meeting Trelayne's gaze, the peasant mustered the last of his strength and wrenched a broken slat from the barrel.

Derik slashed upward, crushing his body against the jagged wood of his prison. His weapon, feeble though it was, tore across Kilsharne's belly. The spell leapt from her lips unfinished, she staggered back, and fell.

Freed from the magic, Trelayne dragged himself across the floor toward his trapped friend. He levered up the barrel with a broken chair.

Derik scrambled up, raising the knight to his side. "My lord—Trelayne, it's done," he urged, "we have to go."

"I have to be sure she's dead," Trelayne told him. He stumbled to the table and looked where she had fallen.

A trail of blood marked her path, circling to where the dragon's neck hulked through the hole, its scales fading. Huddled by its massive head Kilsharne lay, her pale fingers stroking the ridge above the lusterless eye. Her own eyes dimmed with pain, and with tears.

For a moment, her image flashed before him, not wounded as she was, but weeks ago, the woman who had taken the young knight to her bed, who had shown him such fire. Had it been merely a distraction, as she'd claimed, so that her army of demons could destroy the cities of his king? He could not quite believe that. His own eyes stung, from more than the smoke.

"I'm dead, Trelayne," she sighed. "And magic dies with me."

"I didn't want it like this," he said.

She laughed without sound. "I would not want to live in a world bereft of dragons." Her head sunk to her dragon's scaled cheek.

Derik tugged at him. "My lord, we must go!"

Around them, the building groaned with fire. Burning tapestries fell and lanterns roared and burst. With a last glance toward Loref's body—Loref who had died so that Trelayne could succeed—the knight let himself be led from the chamber, down the rickety stairs into the chill night.

Behind them, the fortress sparked into the sky, the funeral pyre of the last sorceress. A small group of refugees, huddled by their broken wagon, stared past them, daring to hope the battle was over. Wearily, the two companions turned toward the forest and home.

Derik whistled for the horses, steering Trelayne to where the trusted steeds emerged tentatively from the trees. "There they are, my lord."

"They'd not leave us, my friend." Trelayne smiled, a little, until it hurt his scorched cheek, and he let the smile slip away. "After all we've been through, Derik, you are entitled to use my name."

"Hard to break the old habit, my lord," the man replied,

helping him up into the saddle.

"To the east, where Gwenyth awaits."

"Aye, lord, and a nice warm meal."

"And a pint at the pub," Trelayne added, glancing at his companion.

Derik winced, feeling his bruised ribs where the vast keg had struck him down. "I don't know about that, my lord." Then he met Trelayne's eyes and grinned, a grin which quickly broke open into an enormous bray of laughter, his eyes sparked. "We live, my lord—through dragon's fire and magic, yet we live."

"That's magic enough for me." Trelayne reached out to Derik and clasped his right shoulder—the salute of one knight to another. After a moment, his expression solemn, Derik returned the gesture.

Through three days, and four nights they rode, coming up to the gates of Goshan after sunrise. They joined the wagons of farmers coming to market and passed beneath their own familiar wall. Six months had passed; six long months of riding hard and fighting harder, until that terrible night in the sorceress's keep when they struck the last blow which freed them from magic forever. Thank the Gods that they had succeeded before Kilsharne's power spread too far. These citizens never had to fear for their lives, or flee their homes from the onslaught of the magical army.

A few well-dressed lords and ladies raised their hands to greet him as he passed, murmuring their surprise to see him home from the army. The ache of his wounds, though they had been bound with healing herbs, prevented him from any enthusiastic acknowledgment, but his heart rose to see his friends again. Beside him, Derik shrank into his saddle, gazing frequently toward the poorer quarter where his little house waited.

Viceroy Brisson approached, on a magnificent dappled horse, at the head of an outfitted hunting party. "Glad to have you back, Trelayne. Wounds, is it?" the old man asked gruffly, his offered hand trembling and gone slightly yellow.

Trelayne briefly clasped his hand. "Yes, sir, but I'll be well enough when I've had some time to rest."

"In time for my ball, of course," he said sternly. Then the viceroy leaned to look around Trelayne, pinching together his bushy eyebrows. "Who's that then?"

"Derik the wheelwright, sir. He's served beside me." Trelayne gestured for Derik to move up beside him again, and frowned when the man made no move, but only let his gaze slide away.

The viceroy humphed. "Beside you? Some strange arrangements in the army, what?"

Trelayne blinked, trying to cut through the mist of pain which hovered in his vision. "Well, I needed a good man, and there's none—" his horse suddenly sprang forward, and, by the time he had controlled it again, the mayor's party had ridden on. He glanced back to find Derik catching up on his smaller horse, slipping his dagger back into its sheath.

"Perhaps I'd best be going home, my lord, if I've your leave."

The flank of Trelayne's horse bore a little fleck of blood, as if it had been pricked by something. His eyes narrowed.

"Something's wrong, Derik. What is it?"

"Just that I should be going home." He nodded over his shoulder where the tall houses gave way to ragged huts. "As should you, my lord. After all, Gwenyth is waiting."

"That she is, my friend. I'll see you at the Lion's Den?"

Derik shrugged noncommittally. "Depends on my mother, if she's been well in my absence, my lord."

"I wish her good health," Trelayne offered. Then he leaned over from his horse, gritting his teeth against the protest of his body, and squeezed Derik's shoulder.

After a moment's hesitation, Derik did the same, his grubby fingers pressing gently. His soft brown eyes met Trelayne's startling blue, and he returned the fierce grin, but his brows drooped, and the shadows there were deep.

Trelayne turned his mount's head toward the hill, trotting along the wide paved street toward the grand hall near the top of it, where the lady Gwenyth lived. To the right, by the wall, the gallows hill rose up, topped with the device of execution. A body dangled there, while crows flapped about, squawking for their supper. When the Magistrate had made his point, they'd bury the body beneath the gallows field. Trelayne turned away, gazing at the citadel which dominated the city. Towers sprang up, bright flags waving in the wind. The citadel served both as the viceroy's elegant home, and also the city's military center, teeming with soldiers on its mid-level, and with prisoners in its deepest bowels. At the foot of its granite walls stood the hall of his beloved. When he entered the courtyard, several grooms appeared, bowing their heads to him, and helped him dismount. Eagerly,

Trelayne limped up the stairs, calling for Gwenyth.

At the head of the stairs, Bessie, the aging housekeeper, curtseyed to him. "Young Master, we did not expect you," she said, her hands fluttering against her skirt.

"The war's done, Bessie." He craned his neck to look beyond her. "Where's Gwenyth?"

"She has guests, my lord. Perhaps you'd like to rest, and change from your travel clothes?" Bessie's head bobbed as she eyed his torn and bloody garments.

"I thought I'd never see her again, Bess, and I refuse to wait one moment longer." Trelayne pushed past toward the wide, bright hall. "Gwenyth? Gwenyth!" he called into the formal rooms at the back of the house. "Gwen—there you are!" He pushed open the double doors to the Rose Parlor and limped through into the sunlit brilliance of elegant rugs and silk cushions.

Gwenyth sprang to her feet, face pale. Her guests remained seated, the four ladies clutching their parasols, while the men turned to stare at the source of the interruption.

Leaning against the door, Trelayne paused to compose himself. His knee throbbed, and he saw that the bandage had slipped, letting a few drops of blood fall onto the wool of the rug. He bent to adjust the bandage, biting his lip. How had he forgotten how beautiful she was? Mastering his emotions, Trelayne moved toward his beloved, his hand reaching out for hers.

Blinking, Gwenyth took a tiny step back, her yellow satin skirts gathered in both hands.

"It's not as bad as it looks, Gwen. The healers say I'll be all right—even my eyebrows will grow back." Trelayne touched his scorched skin with a hopeful finger. "I may not dance so well, though. I'm sorry." His leg twitched with the pain of standing, and his hand still hovered in the air.

Her face composed itself slowly not into the compassion he anticipated, but into a sort of pleasant blandness usually reserved for small children with whom she had lost patience. "I did not expect you, Trelayne, certainly not like this."

"Didn't I promise I'd be back in time for the Viceroy's ball?" He grinned. "I've two months to recover before then. Besides, I had to see you." Indeed, his eyes drank in her glorious blonde hair, her trim, lovely figure, the delicate hands which played the harp with such feeling. Despite the impropriety, he longed to kiss every part of her. Through every battle, even while he lay in Kilsharne's bed, it was Gwenyth's image that gave him strength and hope. Now, the image turned to reality, nearly overcoming him. He put out his other hand to catch himself upon a bookstand as his body swayed.

The ladies gasped, and one of the men stood up, Sir Richard, the captain of the city guard, and Trelayne's one-time sword master. "Now see here, Trelayne, you're frightening the ladies."

A pang of sorrow crossed Gwenyth's face and she came toward him, tall and graceful. She leaned around him, careful not to touch his soiled clothing, and glared down at the manuscript upon the stand. Grime from the road, and flecks of Trelayne's blood speckled the pages. She turned her face up to his, and hissed, "You could at least have washed your face before barging in on my and my guests. Is this the way you intend to act as my husband?"

Trelayne's outstretched hand fell to his side. "I—I am sorry, Love. I didn't think—"

"No, you certainly did not," she returned, wrinkling her nose at the smell of him.

"I've been at war," he whispered. "I nearly died."

"Ah—so the war is reason enough to lose all your manners? You are a gentleman, or had you forgotten?"

Her narrowed eyes and thin lips confronted him. "You don't understand, Gwenyth, it wasn't just a war. The enemy were demons, with a dragon at their head, and—"

She snorted. "I can't talk to you when you're like this." Pulling back, she crossed her arms, then her hand shot out to his chest, she plucked at a shred of fabric. "This is the shirt I stitched for you." Beneath the stains, the embroidered birds and flowers were barely visible.

"I wore it for courage."

"You were supposed to wear it on our wedding day." Gwenyth turned her back and crossed toward her guests. "I do apologize for Trelayne's behavior. Apparently his wounds have addled his mind. Please forgive the interruption."

"But is he all right?" one of the men asked.

"He assures me he will be fine, and will be ready for dinner this evening." She shot an arch glance over her shoulder.

Dazed, Trelayne nodded once, accepting the off-hand invitation. Taking a deep breath, he pushed off from the wood, and stumbled back through the door. He nearly bowled over a servant with a water bucket who had begun scrubbing at the bloodstains down the hall.

Going at last to his own home, Trelayne found his parents had gone off for their annual summer pilgrimage, this time to the temple of Ishdren in the distant mountains. Quietly, he submitted to the scrubbing of a manservant, and the chiding of their household healer. Finally, they left him and he was able to tumble into his bed.

A timid prod awakened Trelayne some hours later, to get him up for the dinner to come. His clothes had already been laid out for him—a tunic with puffed sleeves utterly impractical for anything, and stockings that were sure to reveal the lumps of bandages beneath. "This won't work," he groaned. "Give me something longer, and a cane." The rest, welcome though it had been, aroused all sorts of pain when he stood again.

"That'd be completely unfashionable, my lord," the servant said, shaking his head. "Besides which, you asked me yourself to clean out the old clothes from your wardrobe. Only the latest, you said before you left."

"Would I have said that?" Trelayne glanced around his own room. In his absence, the velvet curtains and throws of winter had been changed for the lighter look of spring, and the round-toed shoes of last year had been replaced with narrow, pointed things. Vaguely, he recalled the orders he had left, wanting to be ready for the festivals of summer, the parties of autumn with Gwenyth at his side. It all seemed so distant.

He allowed the man to dress him, wincing when the

stockings were pulled up over his wounds. He was forced to reject the shoes, in favor of his rather shabby boots. His knee demanded at least that concession. The servant held up a tall mirror for him, and Trelayne winced. He saw now why Gwenyth and her guests had looked so aghast. Dragon's fire had singed the right side of his face, and taken his eyebrows with it, leaving him a queer mix of angry red and fading tan—ghastly indeed. He could not smile properly, but produced only a lop-sided leer. His hands snaked with scars from the dragon's blood, looking as if he'd bound his fingers up with threads. Nonetheless, until he'd had a chance to heal, he would have to do.

A carriage brought Trelayne again to his lady's door, bright with lanterns and music. Sighing, he accepted a footman's hand down from the carriage, and moved stiffly up the steps. Inside the bustling hall, Trelayne found Gwenyth in the midst of a mob of the older ladies, laughing and receiving advice.

"Oh, Trelayne," one of them cooed, distracting him from Gwenyth's approving smile, "How was the war? Did you do anything brave?"

His mind flashed to an image of Loref, dueling the dragon with only a broken spear while Trelayne scrambled for his sword. His friend's dying shriek echoed still in his ears, and he shuddered. "I had some brave friends," he replied.

The ladies tittered, and Gwenyth, coaxed, "Surely you did something to earn your wounds?"

"We were the ones who found the sorceress's keep," he said, watching the scene in his memory. "We had to confront her, and kill the dragon in order to stop the demon army. Loref, Derik and I—"

"I don't recall any Sir Derik," the old lady protested.

"He's a wheelwright, with a strong right arm." He bunched his own muscles, remembering the thrust of the barrel-stave that had saved him.

The ladies laughed uproariously now, Gwenyth joining in. "No really, Darling, what happened?"

"I'm telling you," he snapped back. "The units were all confused, knights with pike men, it didn't matter, when we were set upon by demons. Derik saved my life, more than once, and Loref—"

"Now who's he?"

"He was a half-orc, a scout for the king—" the indrawn breath all around him stopped the words in his throat, and he awoke to the stares and revulsion in their faces. After the last great war against magic, the Orc War, twenty years ago, women came forward who had been ravaged by the vile invaders. Their misshapen children were taken up in the army since few other paths were open to them. "Yes," he replied to their astonished expressions, "I rode with an orc, and he was the bravest one among us. We needed him for his resistance to magic."

"But this is a modern country, Trelayne," Gwenyth pointed out, "there isn't any magic."

"Not for a long time," he agreed, "but Kilsharne found a way to wake a dragon, she was bringing magic back into the world, with the help of her demons."

"Her?" Gwenyth's expression was innocent, but a spark

leapt in her eyes.

Holding up a hand, he said, "Wait, let me tell it in order."

"Oh, no, I want to hear about this woman. You went to her keep, you said?"

"Yes," he stammered, "Yes, I did, but she—"

Gwenyth slapped him, her palm smacking a jolt of pain through his scorched cheek that shivered all the way through his aching body. "Get out of my house," she hissed.

"If you'd just listen, Gwen." His head reeled, and his vision swam.

"I've heard enough, oh great adventurer. You shall not make a mockery of me in front of my friends."

Trelayne stumbled back, nearly fell down the stairs, but he managed to catch himself and headed for the street. Half-blind with pain, he made his way to the Lion's Den, bursting through the doors to catch himself on a table. He collapsed into a chair to catch his breath, glancing around at the rough faces that were already turning back to their drinks.

"—so I says, you were trapped under a barrel, during the whole fight with the dragon?" the drunken speaker guffawed, interrupting his own story, "and he says, yeah, I was, and I says, ye're not even sober enough make yerself the hero?" He rapped his skull with his meaty fingers.

Hoots of laughter followed this observation, and Trelayne wobbled to his feet. "You," he cried, pointing to the man, "are a treacherous lout."

Caught mid swallow, the man turned, eyes round to stare at the young nobleman. He swallowed quickly and said, "Sorry t' bother ye, m'lord, we'll be more quiet, eh?"

"You spoke of Derik the wheelwright, did you not?" Anger flamed beneath Trelayne's skin, tingling in the dragonblood scars.

"Derik the drunkard," the man returned, "What's he to you?"

"He's the man who saved my life, and I'll not hear a word against him, not from the likes of you."

"An' what's that mean, then? I'm beneath the likes of him? 'Fore he went to war, the bastard hadn't mended a wheel in months, he was so busy workin' on the drink!"

"It doesn't matter a damn what he was before, he is my friend."

The man's drink burst from his lips as he hollered with renewed laughter. "Yer friend, is he? That's the best one I've heard all night, my lord. Tell us another!" He pounded the table in his mirth.

Trelayne staggered as he threw the punch, but it still caught the man hard on the cheek, sending him sprawling.

His opponent came up roaring, with a trail of blood at his lip. His fists flew before he thought, knocking the wind out of Trelayne and battering him to the floor before his friends caught hold of him and dragged him off.

"Oh, Gods, m'lord, I never meant, oh, please," the big man blubbered, instantly sober. "Are ye hurt? Oh, Sweet Lady."

Squinting through his pain, Trelayne watched the display. His opponent's face had no color as he knelt down, mouth hanging open like the mouth of that dead man on the gallows. The man jerked as he heard a sound from the street:

# Elaine Isaak

the orderly marching of city guards. Sucking in a breath, Trelayne wheezed, "Get me out the back."

"Oh, Gods, I never meant to hurt you, my lord," the man pleaded.

"I know that," Trelayne said, struggling to get himself up. "If they find me like this, they'll kill you. Come on." He urged the man closer with one hand.

At last understanding, the peasant slid his arm across Trelayne's shoulders and helped him, as carefully as he could, out the back door even as guards burst through the front. Lowering Trelayne to the ground, the man quickly pulled off his shirt, and made a pillow of it. "Thank you, my lord, thank you," he repeated as he tried to make the nobleman comfortable. "What can I do? Should I go to your house?"

Trelayne managed a shake of his head. "More trouble that way," he mumbled. "Derik."

"Derik, aye, my lord." He ran off into the night.

A few minutes later, the wheelwright's broad familiar face leaned over him, lit by a small lantern. "What're you doing here, then, my lord?" He laid a careful hand on Trelayne's brow, a shaking hand.

"Looking for you."

"Ye shouldn't have done it. Besides which," Derik glowered at the pub's door, "I'm off the stuff, for good. You need rest. Hasn't your fine lady taken care of you, my lord?"

A small, derisive laugh. "Not so kindly as that man who fetched you."

"I'll go for your housemen, my lord."

Trelayne caught Derik's shoulder and held him. "I'm nobody's lord, Derik, least of all yours."

15

"What're you saying, my lord? You can't stay here."

Thinking of Gwenyth, Trelayne replied, "That much is sure, my friend. But where to go?"

"What're you saying?" Derik repeated, but he settled himself at Trelayne's head, and kept his hand placed softly there.

"I have fought demons, and stood up to a dragon." He smiled lopsidedly into the lamplight. "How much harder it seems to fight fashion, and stand up to gossip. You fought beside me, back there, but here, you're expected to walk behind me, and never meet my eyes."

Derik's averted gaze flashed up. "You're a lord, Trelayne," he said sharply, "I'm a peasant."

"Here, we are, but out there? We have been adventurers together."

"Oh, no," Derik shook his head. "You want to leave? After all we've done to save our home, you want to ride off again?"

"How's your mother?"

Derik gave his bray of laughter, as jarring as it was welcome. "Her crotchety self."

"Well then?"

The peasant cocked his head toward the wounded knee. "You're hurt, Trelayne."

"I'm better by the minute," he responded, pushing himself to sit up, then waiting for the dizziness to pass as Derik shook his head, supporting Trelayne with his strong arm.

"You're mad, too, Trelayne, have I told you?"

"Better madness," said Trelayne, standing with the help of his friend, "than to live in a world bereft of dragons."

# CHAPTER

# TWO

### *A Life in Trade*

TRELAYNE AWOKE TO FULL SUN on his face, coming through a mysterious window he did not recall having. He rubbed his weary eyes and stretched cautiously, vaguely surprised to find his chest naked. The bed didn't feel right either, as he patted it with aching fingers: lumpy, with a coarse coverlet, not satin. He squinted up again at the light, and remembered the night before, someone hauling him up the ladder. The sun streamed in through a chink in a thatched roof. He must be lying in a loft over one of the cottages, Derik's, presumably. All below was quiet.

Trelayne pushed off the woolen blankets and inspected his legs. Someone had kindly dressed him in a pair of workman's trews, loose enough not to bind the fresh bandages he discovered on his right knee. Rolling gently to

17

his left, Trelayne peered down into the cottage. The single room held a rude table and a pair of benches, one of them occupied by a ragged gray cat which eyed him indifferently. Tools and sacks hung from pegs on the wall, and cooking pots from the stone of the fireplace, with a tall cupboard to one side. The end wall, which he could barely make out through the gloom, was closed off by a curtain—probably a sleeping alcove. The entire house would have fit into his bedchamber back home.

Trelayne winced. Home. He had felt lost among the finery, trying to remember what his life had been. Before the demons, he recalled a swirl of parties, picnics, the sort of lessons befitting a gentleman—most of these in recent months, with the lovely Gwenyth at his side. Lovely, and empty, in a way he could just begin to grasp. When he summoned her to mind, now, the saw her disapproving stare as he stood bleeding on her exquisite rugs, offering his hand. He shut his eyes, and took a deep breath.

Below, the ill-fitting door popped open, and a dark head stuck through, looking up. Derik's face split in a broad grin. "So you're up, then?"

"Awake, at least, but not much more."

"There's porridge in the pot—not what you're used to, I reckon."

"Gods, I haven't eaten since you and I broke bread yesterdawn."

"Get down here," Derik called up, then hesitated, watching, with his mouth slightly open. He looked a little foolish, and it took Trelayne a moment to realize that the other man wasn't sure he could get down the ladder, and, at the same time, wasn't sure how to ask.

Giving the lop-sided smile that spared his cheek, Trelayne scooted over to the ladder, and set his foot on it. The right leg wouldn't bear his full weight, but he managed to hang onto the rungs and let himself down without a tumble. Nodding grimly, he hobbled to the door.

Derik stepped back into the open court, gesturing broadly. "My domain," he said, with a shrug of his big shoulders, "such as it is."

Outside to the right grew a small patch of tangled vegetables, beans and parsnips vying for the light. To the left, the yard was littered with wagon wheels in various states of repair. Jigs of wood and iron held the curves of rims, while a narrow carving bench with a foot-operated wooden vise gripped the start of a spoke. Weeds choked the jumble of tools and materials.

Surveying the mess, Derik's shoulders drooped. "Miller was right when he said I'd not worked in too long."

"That was the miller?"

"Aye, Roger, the one who took a swing at you." Derik chuckled. "Oh, he's right eager to apologize all over again."

"He only gave what he got," Trelayne remarked. "It's not worth dying for."

Derik cocked his head, wearing that curious frown that only touched his eyes. "Not many like you," he said at last.

Trelayne eyed him sidelong, unsure what to say to this. Instead of answering, he studied the scene around him. To both sides of the wheelwright's cluttered yard stood cottages as tattered and tilted as his, with barrels and crates stacked along the walls. Across the street of mud and straw, a narrow alley threaded among the houses back toward the city proper. The two cottages forming its entrance were joined by a series of rods, with great loops of thread dangling down, dripping a rainbow of dyes.

"Dye-mistress over there, and a weaver next door. Good neighbors, all," Derik said gruffly. "But you'll be going home, today, I reckon." He folded his arms, casting his gaze to the wreckage of his work.

"What about our adventures?" Trelayne asked lightly. In the bare brilliance of daylight, he could feel the throbbing of his wounds, and the pinch of the scorched skin of his face, which had had no chance to heal.

"You really think we should go?" Derik shook his head, his dark tail of hair twitching along his spine. "And you in that condition? We'd not get a mile."

"Very well, then, we'll bide our time." He tapped his leg. "The cut's not so deep; maybe in a couple of weeks, I'll be good to ride."

The dark tail bobbed up and down with a curt nod. "Get on home then. Best I don't go with you."

Trelayne's pale toes kneaded the straw on the doorstep. "I don't think I can do that. It's not my home anymore."

"Oh, for love of the Lady! What're you saying?" Derik rounded on him, drawing himself up, though the top of his head still reached no further than Trelayne's chin. "What other home've you got? And there's that lady waiting—"

"Not any more. She broke it off," Trelayne snapped. "We

did, last night."

Derik grunted, a sound that lifted his shoulders in question.

"She couldn't understand about the war, that it wasn't for glory, that I didn't spend the last six months rubbing shoulders with the cream of western nobility. She doesn't believe in the demons." He sighed, "I can't talk to her."

"So that's it," Derik said flatly.

"After six months apart, she wouldn't welcome me until I'd cleaned and changed. Well, I have changed!" he exploded, his hands flying up in the air. "I've changed so much she doesn't even recognize me." He brought his hands down more slowly, examining his palms roughened by the hilt of his sword, and the narrow red scars of dragon's blood twining around his fingers. "I don't recognize me."

Derik's dark eyes roved over the young man's face. "Where'll you go, then?"

With a rueful twitch of a smile, Trelayne said, "You're the only other friend I have in the world."

Lips curling, Derik snorted a chuckle. Then he let go, the braying laughter shaking his body down to his mended boots. "Gods, Trelayne, what kind of friend am I? Look at this place!" He spread his arms to take in the mess in the yard, the dung in the street. "You're used to parlors and featherbeds, and servants, for mercy's sake!"

Trelayne stiffened to stone. "Listen to me carefully, Derik, for I will not say this again." Every word rang with cold precision. "Whoever I might have been, I am not that man."

"Who are you then?" Derik asked quietly.

"I don't know yet. I'm asking for time to find out. Please don't ask me to go back to that life." His face softened, the blue eyes shaded.

Derik shifted his weight from one foot to the other, his mouth shifting, too, as he considered. "If you're to stay with me," he said at last, "you'll need to earn your keep."

"Yes, of course." Relief broke over his face, and Derik couldn't help but return the smile.

"Curse you for an innocent fool, Trelayne," he muttered.

"Maybe so," Trelayne agreed. "Tell me what to do."

"First, eat something. Then help me clean up this wreck and make it a proper yard."

Limping inside, Trelayne fell upon his bowl of porridge as if he'd never had anything so divine. The next three days, they spent pulling weeds and polishing tools. Derik hauled away some of the supplies too rotted or rusted for use, refusing Trelayne's assistance. "Rest that leg, or you're no good to me."

The neighbors watched him curiously, but asked no questions, and Derik gave no explanation. Trelayne had the distinct impression that they were more shocked by the clean-up of the yard than by his own presence there, and the miller's story seemed to have gotten around. Derik's aging mother slept in the curtained alcove, and made daily rounds of every temple in the quarter. At her slow pace, she often did not return until near dark. She nodded to Trelayne, but spoke barely at all as she got the men's meager supper. After an evening of jokes or tales, they slept in the loft, under a heap of blankets as they'd done on the road from Kilsharne's keep.

Though his tasks were mostly sedentary, the day's labor left Trelayne tired and eager for his bed. Still, after that first night, he dreaded it as well, for the images it brought. Sometimes Kilsharne slew him in her bed, and sometimes it was Gwenyth who died in Kilsharne's place. More often, he fell beneath the bulk of the dragon, screaming as it flamed, screaming all the more when Loref appeared, bellowing, and the dragon rent him open from chin to crotch. Trelayne woke shuddering, unsure if the screams had been dream or reality. Derik's snoring assured him he was safe and silent, but Trelayne fingered his hoarse throat in the mornings, and wondered if his friend's sleep was a potion or a lie.

When he was satisfied that the yard and tools would serve, Derik set about to teach Trelayne his trade. He sat him down on the carving bench, and pressed a drawknife into his hands. "Take a split—"he plucked a narrow piece of wood from the pile readily to hand—"lock it in the vise, and carve it round." He held up the spoke he had just demonstrated.

Trelayne gamely took a split, and tucked it into the upper mouth of the vise. He pressed the foot pedal below to hold it, and set upon it with the fervor of a young beaver.

Derik laughed over his shoulder for a minute, then said, "Well, keep it up! I've got to see if I can get us some business, or the larder'll be bare by Sunday."

By sunset, Trelayne had a large pile of wood shavings, and a handful of crooked spokes. Derik, shoulders drooping, clapped him on the back with a weary smile. "You'll get it, given time. Better luck tomorrow."

He didn't talk of his own luck, and Trelayne nodded absently.

The next day, they both renewed their tasks, and Trelayne tested himself by letting his right leg take some of the pressure of holding the vise. Every day stronger. He smiled as he worked.

As the sun rose high, sweat trickled down his bare, bronzed back, and he had to pause often to wipe the dripping hair from his face. Shaving his face aggravated the burns, so he had abandoned that in favor of a scruffy beard. He scratched under his chin, rolling his shoulders back as he sat up straight for the first time since morning.

Across the way, the young weaver stepped from her door, reaching up to check the new lot of dyed wool. Smiling to herself, she turned back, and noticed him. The weaver wore a tunic which clung a little to her body, and drew in at the waist under a skirt of rusty brown. Unlike those of the ladies, the peasant's skirts ended at her calf, revealing a strong ankle and delicate toes. Trelayne quickly drew his eyes back up again, and met her gaze. She shook back her dark brown hair, and let him look.

"Good morrow, wheelwright," she called, a hint of laughter in her voice.

"And a good day to you, weaver," he answered.

"Trelayne, is it not?"

"Aye, it is. And you'd be Anmoria."

"That I would." She crossed her arms beneath her breasts. "Bring you a sip from the well? I'm headed that way."

"I'd be most glad of it, my lady." The last words tacked on out of long habit.

Anmoria laughed gaily. "Keep your fancy talk, I'll have none of it." She vanished down the alley, and returned a moment later with an earthenware pitcher. Crossing the muddy street and jumping the trickling channel, she came to stand beside him.

Trelayne politely rose, and was rewarded with another laugh, another flash of her smile.

"No goblets here, sir," she teased. "We'll have to share."

She held up the pitcher for him, and he accepted it, taking a long draught before he gave it back. The cold spring water soothed the heat of his body—well, most of it—and he reflected that water, offered with a smile, tasted sweeter to him than wine.

Swallowing her own cool mouthful, Anmoria shrugged her farewell, and made her way back across the street to her loom.

"Thanks," he called to her back, watching the sway of her hips as she jumped the stream.

With a smile still on his lips, he went back to work, and created his first perfect spoke.

# CHAPTER

## THREE

### *Temple of Secrets*

THE WATER-SHARING BECAME ANOTHER RITUAL in this spare life he was adjusting to. Though he offered to do the fetching, Anmoria refused him, saying it stretched her legs. Trelayne had to admit the few times he'd walked as far as the well had set his knee to groaning, and he wasn't sure the pitcher would make it back whole.

Derik found them a few jobs, and grinned at his new apprentice's progress. A fortnight later, they had completed a new set of wheels for a wine merchant, and Derik gleefully hauled the lot off, talking of the feast they'd have that night.

Lounging on his bench, idly fingering the latest spoke, Trelayne stiffened at the sound of marching feet. They approached from the city, four guardsmen on official business, from the look of them. So far, Trelayne had managed to avoid meeting the guard by hiding out in the alcove whenever they came by. He gathered that he had been given up for a lunatic by his retainers, and that there would be little fuss made until his parents returned and sought him out. He was about to rise and head inside, when he saw the lead man stride up to Anmoria's door. The scars on his fingers itched fiercely, and, rather than withdraw, he lifted a file, and bent over the spoke.

Soon, all four men had disappeared inside, and a murmur of voices reached him, then shouting. Anmoria tumbled through the door, followed by the captain. Inside, a terrible cracking told him they were tearing her place apart. Trelayne jumped up, the spoke clenched in his fist.

Anmoria scrambled in the mud, struggling for purchase as the captain loomed over her. "I tell you, I haven't got any, not a thread!" she pleaded.

"Little whore," he snarled, grabbing her out-thrust arm. He heaved her up so that her feet dangled. "I'm sick of having to talk to you! Tell me where it is, or I swear you'll get what's coming to you."

Two bounds took Trelayne on shaky legs across the street. "What's going on here?" Slivers from the spoke ground into his palm.

"None of your concern." The guard threw Anmoria aside, into the alley, turning his back on Trelayne. He landed a kick on her chin that sent her sprawling.

Arm raised, Trelayne sprang after them. "Leave her alone!"

"Are you threat—"the man began, turning, but Trelayne

had already struck a heavy blow across the man's helmet.

Rattled, the captain stumbled back, fumbling for his sword.

"Get away, Trelayne." Anmoria pulled herself up, wiping blood from her mouth. "You'll only get yourself hurt."

A strong hand grabbed him, flinging him against the wall, and a sword came up beneath his chin. The guardsman stared him in the eyes. "What'll I do, Captain?"

As the other two emerged and made for Anmoria, the captain bared his teeth at Trelayne, leaning in close. "You're that madman living with the peasants, aren't you? Lucky for you, I'm not hurt, or I'd have plenty of cause, even for you, my lord," he sneered. To the guard, he added, "Just keep him still, I'll be quick about it."

One of the men was standing on Anmoria's wrists, grinding them into the dirt as she struggled. The captain kicked her skirts up over her face, and threw himself down upon her.

"Bastards," Trelayne hissed between clenched teeth.

"What do you care? Just a peasant whore," the man holding him said, pressing close with his ale-drenched breath.

The fourth man came to stand beside them, then leaned casually against the alley wall, looking out toward Derik's.

"Or is that you don't want to share?" the guard sneered.

Cautiously, Trelayne shifted his grip on the spoke, bringing it in close. In a sudden movement, he jerked it up between the guard's legs.

Cursing, the man fell back, pain twisting his face. He

tried to lunge forward, but Trelayne brought the wood down hard across his wrist, snatching the dropped sword from mid-air. He swung backhand, and slashed open the man's belly beneath his breastplate.

The guard holding Anmoria shouted, drawing his own sword and springing to the attack even as his fellow did.

Struggling with his pants, the captain started to rise, so Anmoria's kick caught him square in the chest, slamming his head against the wall.

Trelayne set his back to the wall, fending off blows from both sides.

Ducking suddenly, he dove between them, send a parting blow to one man's ribs with a wicked thrust. He found himself heaped beside the fallen captain, and grabbed the man's shoulders to swing him up as the next blow aimed for his heart.

The guard gasped as his own sword skewered his captain.

Trelayne pushed the body aside and rose to shaky legs, but the man had already set off at a run, calling for reinforcements.

Chest heaving, Trelayne let his weapons fall from his nerveless hands. His eyes found Anmoria, her body clenched, bloody arms wrapped about her knees. He limped over the captain's body. "Anmoria, are you hurt?"

"Get away from me," her voice emerged in an angry curse from beneath the tangle of hair.

"Are you hurt?" he repeated numbly, hands braced on the wall, swaying.

"I would have been fine!" she shot back, whipping

the hair from her face. Blood seeped from her lips. "They would've had their fun, and I'd be fine, now look!" Her torn arm gestured to the dead men in the alley. "Curse you, my lord, you've killed me with this!"

Dumbly, he shook his head. "I killed them, it's my fault; and it was in defense of you. There are laws—"

"In the city, there are laws. Down here? Do you think those laws are made for us? Worthless paper, my lord." Her teeth flashed in a grin of blood. "They'll kill me for spite, and let you walk with a chiding."

Trelayne slid down the wall, his aching leg stuck out while the other crumpled with him. "I wanted to help you," he murmured.

"You could've helped me better by staying away." Anmoria yanked her skirts in place, spattering them with blood and straw.

"Oh, Gods," he whispered.

Painfully, Anmoria pulled herself up. She searched desperately one way, then the other. "Get up and run, they'll be here soon."

Trelayne's palms were pressed to his eyes, but could not hold in the tears. "I'm sorry," he moaned, "I'm sorry, I…" the words trailed off.

Anmoria's fists clenched, then released, trembling. She hunched down beside him. "Trelayne," she breathed, "get up." When he did not move, she gently stroked the tears from the darkness which still marred his cheek. "Oh, Trelayne, I don't know how to be saved; no one ever tried before you." Carefully, she pried his hands from his face, gripping them tightly. Tears and shadows ravaged his face; the blue eyes squeezed shut. "Come with me," she whispered, drawing him up. Together, limping, and clinging to each other, they ran into the darkening day.

Trelayne stumbled often on the long, crazy flight through the rabbit warren of the quarter. They careered around corners at unexpected angles, avoiding the most populous areas, except for a sprint across the edge of the market where vendors were packing up the remnants of their wares.

They stopped at last before a tall, narrow door flanked by two falcons carved in stone. Their inlaid yellow eyes stabbed at Trelayne as he followed Anmoria into the darkness. On the other side, they did not pause, but shuffled down a cold, unlit hall, one hand to the stone, the other still holding on. The floor slanted down, and Anmoria hissed, "Careful—stairs."

They descended for what seemed like hours, and Trelayne finally saw a light ahead, the flickering glow of torches. The smoke swirled upward, and he coughed, inhaling the burning odor, and another breath of decay. He swallowed hard as his feet struck level ground. The room lifted away above them to a domed roof, flickering with gold work in a mosaic jungle. Trelayne caught his breath, captivated by the dancing beauty of the ancient motifs—white herons, gleaming butterflies, and brilliant flowers writhed about the stone ceiling. At the center, a human figure drifted on golden clouds, a dark woman with eyes on her palms, always watching.

Anmoria gazed up with him, her breathing slowing to

normal. She even managed a smile as she brought her palms together, and raised them to the lady on the ceiling. "The Blue Lady," she murmured.

"But she's—"

"Heresy, my lord, is that what you'd say?" a new voice croaked.

Trelayne found the speaker parting a curtain on the opposite side of the round chamber. The old woman's eyes were pale white orbs, unwavering. She opened the ruin of her mouth to reveal a few near-black teeth. Humped with age, she might reach to his chest, but no further. Her clawed hands wrapped the handle of a cane as straight as she herself seemed twisted. Slowly, she inclined her head, and raised it again. "You find me repulsive," she said, the voice again like a scratching of branches.

"I—"he began, then squared himself. "Yes, Granny, but I do not yet know you."

She cackled, offering again her ragged smile. "Trelayne, is it? The son of Marshall and Imogene, their only. You wonder how I can know you, my lord."

"I do."

"The Blue Lady's temple has not always been forbidden. A few years after your birth, only. Before that, mothers trusted me to listen to their wombs, to speak the chants of blessing, as I did for you." She held out a beckoning hand. "Come here, let me see you."

Anmoria gave him a little push, and Trelayne did as she bid him. Standing before her, he realized she meant to touch him, to see him with her crabbed hands. Clenching his teeth,

32

he knelt before her.

Her lips drooped in a frown. "Not so healed as you thought, my lord, that cut from the demon blade."

"No, Granny," he sighed, eyes shut as he struggled to master the pain.

Her hand reached out to him then, settling like a feather upon his brow. His eyebrows had grown back, but dark, not the flashing gold of the rest of his hair. Her crooked thumb gently stroked the new hairs. So close, he felt the moisture of her breath upon him, smelled the rot of her teeth. Then, in a thin voice, she began to sing. The wordless melody rose up from some deep place within her, as her fingers gently moved across his face. Eyes shut, he sighed at their unexpected softness. The tension ebbed from his face, drew down his rigid back, spreading warmth.

Her tune became words, strange, yet soothing, in a language he did not know. Still they echoed within him, tugging at some distant memory, then letting it subside. His breathing steadied, and the pain of the demon wound receded to a dull ache. As softly as they had come, her fingers drew away.

"Rest you tonight, Trelayne," the creaky voice told him, and it sounded less grating on his ears.

The priestess rustled past them, and Anmoria once again helped him up, bringing him through the curtain into a series of living chambers. "We'll be safe here, for a while."

"Was that magic?" he breathed, still under the peace of the old woman's song.

"It might be," Anmoria replied calmly. "If it is, it is the

last. And it's part of why the Lady is out of favor. Granny Falcon is the last of her priestesses in the city." She drew aside the curtain of a sleeping alcove, then winced at the pain.

"You need to clean those scratches," Trelayne said wearily.

"Don't you think I know that?" Instantly, she frowned at herself. "I don't mean to hurt you, I just. . . it's been a very hard day."

"I know," he whispered. "I'm sorry."

She shrugged. "Get some sleep, I'll take care of myself." She pushed him gently, but firmly onto the bed.

For a while, he lay awake, listening to the splash of water, and her muffled curses as the cleansing stung. Trelayne let himself drift, and finally let go of consciousness.

# Chapter Four

### *Lord and Madman*

He walked again the long hall to Kilsharne's keep, sword gripped in his sweaty palm, Derik to his left, Loref straight ahead, his hunched figure and shaggy hair betraying his parentage. Even so, one of the best soldiers Trelayne knew.

"Demons," Loref hissed, his nostrils flaring. He shifted his hands on the haft of his ax, and sniffed again. "Five, maybe six."

"Where?"

"Dead ahead." The half-orc gave a toothy smile, revealing the thick tusks of his canines. "Sorry."

"Can you smell her?" Trelayne couldn't bear to speak her name, not since the morning she'd left him in her bed, left him to go command her demons.

They turned a corner in the hall, and a snarl greeted them.

The demons swung their huge heads, saliva dripping from the fangs bared in their vicious perversion of a smile. The one in the lead spread its tattered vestigial wings, tail lashing. It drew a curved blade which gleamed with unearthly light. Roaring, the demons fell upon them.

Killing the leader with a lucky slash, Trelayne found himself tangled in those leathery wings, slashing over and over to escape them, the foul blackness of them smothering him. He felt the sting of the blade lay open his knee, and screamed.

He jolted awake, a scream dying in his throat and Anmoria's face bathed in a cloud of candlelight. Her other hand clutched his arm. "Are you all right?"

"Yes," he gasped, "yes, fine."

A little smile creased her cheek. "You're an awful liar, Trelayne." She set down the candle on a shelf by his head, but did not release her warm grip on his arm. "Is it you I've been hearing sometimes, late at night?"

"Oh, Gods," he groaned, wiping a hand over his face. "I didn't know it carried that far."

She shook her head, perching on the edge of the sleeping shelf. "I come here to services of the Lady on certain nights. Sometimes I thought I heard something, when I was walking by Derik's door."

"I hope I didn't wake you," he murmured, seeing the dark of bruises blooming on her skin. She needed rest at least as much as he, for what she'd been through.

"For mercy's sake, the way you apologize, anyone'd think you caused a world of trouble." The gripping hand ease to a slight pressure, stroking his upper arm.

"I'm sor—"he shut his mouth on the words, dismissing them with a quick shake of the head.

"You're sorry," she supplied. "I know." The smile slipped from her face. "Why were you screaming?"

He hesitated, recalling the disbelief on Gwenyth's face at the mention of demons, then shrugged one shoulder. "The war," he said. "That's all."

"Haven't I warned you about your lying?"

"I saw things during the war—terrible things—and sometimes, they haunt my dreams. That's all," he finished, a little more firmly this time.

"The devil it is!" She pushed away from the bed, her figure receding into the darkness. "What, do you think I don't know about pain? Or is it that war's not a woman's subject?" Her wild motion stopped, leaving her distant voice their only connection. "Or is a peasant whore not good enough for your secrets?"

His mouth twitched, and his eyes burned. Words of protest died in his throat, for he knew they would come out in a sob.

"That's it, is it? Just another damn lord playing peasant, that's what I get?" her voice clawed at him from the darkness. "Well," she started, coming up to lean over him, her face a mask of fury, but the retort never came. She studied him a moment, her bandaged arms crossed loosely.

"I've never seen a lord cry," she murmured, "not until you. I never thought a lord had cause to weep."

Trelayne shrugged one shoulder, turning his face from

her.

Anmoria lay a hand upon his naked back, but he flinched away. "I was to be married, before the war," he said, wiping furiously at his eyes. "I tried to tell her, when I got back. Gods, I so needed her to hear me."

"What happened?"

A bitter laugh. "I bled on her carpets," he said, "I embarrassed her friends, and then I ruined her party."

"I don't have any carpets, Trelayne." The cushions sank a little, as she settled by the pillow, her warmth radiating to his back. "And I won't have any parties."

He nodded, a pained jerk of the head, his scarred palms covered his eyes.

Anmoria pressed herself against him, her cloth-bandaged arms slipping about his chest, her face nestled against his shoulder. She embraced him as if he would fall apart, as if his shaking were from the cold and she would keep it away with the shield of herself. "Granny said it was a demon sword that cut you," Anmoria murmured, her voice as much a tremor within him as a sound to reach his ears.

"Aye," he said, "the demons rose, for magic was reborn." Haltingly, never looking at her, he told the whole story, even to Kilsharne's seduction, the way the three companions had pursued her, leaving the king's armies to fight her demons, and finally caught her in the keep where her dragon waited. He was not sure he could speak of Loref, of the half-orc's sacrifice, but the words came, and she said nothing; a sigh, a gasp, or a tightening of her arms told him that she heard every word until at last, they ran dry.

For a long time, they sat that way.

"You are a hero," she said at length, "you and Derik both."

He laughed, with a little less bitterness. "Nobody knows what we've done." He shrugged slightly. "I suppose the king, by now, has sorted it out. As far as everyone here knows, it was a war as any other, knights and lords strutting their horses on hilltops while the infantry pike men get slaughtered down below, until the lords on both sides lay aside their differences."

"But you never told anyone until now."

"All we wanted, at the end, was to come home and find our homes safe, unchanged—"a long sigh. "It never occurred to us then that we had changed, that home might offer no place for us."

"And that's why you came to Derik's, and why he lets you stay," she said in a tone of wonder.

"I don't know why he lets me stay. I'm a hopeless wheelwright."

"It didn't occur to you that he needs you as much as you need him? Who does he have but his mother? And you just told me what happened when he told the tale at the pub. Derik left here as a lazy drunkard, slipping by on sufferance. I've never seen him stand so tall as when you stood beside him."

"Doomed to be hopeless together."

They sat still a while longer.

"Are you ready for some rest?" she asked, raising her head. "I know I am."

He twisted carefully from her arms, facing her in the

dim light. "Will you stay, Anmoria?"

She held his face in her hands, and pressed her lips to his brow. "Until you sleep, I'll stay, and I won't be far away."

Trelayne lay back on the pillow, and Anmoria lay beside him, stroking his hair, until the warmth of sleep had taken him.

He awoke alone, and shivering. Reaching for the blankets jumbled at his feet, he thought he heard voices. Trelayne gathered a blanket over his shoulders as a cloak and climbed from the alcove. His knee put up only a token protest, and he made his way in the direction of both sound and light. A gathering had assembled in the round chamber, a dozen or more people struggling to keep their voices quiet, despite the emotions that rose in them.

"Well, he should never have taken in a lord, that's what I say—and a madman at that!" A strident female voice spoke up.

"What's he t'do? The man's saved his life, and he's returned the favor. Ye don't know what the war'll do to a man." A familiar guttural tone, but Trelayne couldn't place it.

"I don't see why we should concern ourselves at all. Derik's been no friend to me," grumped a younger man.

"Gods, lad, he's one of us, and the war's served him better. Not a drop of wine nor ale, I'll swear it, not since that night i' the Den he tried to tell us."

"Roger's right," Anmoria put in. "They're both telling the same tale, and they've the scars to prove it."

"Oh, you'd know, would you, dearie?" another woman said.

Trelayne pushed aside the curtain and barged in. Anmoria jumped up from a cushion by the stairs, and came to his side, her face anxious. "You should rest."

"As should you," he told her, then looked beyond her to the worried faces around the room, "but it sounds as if we're both needed here. What's the trouble?"

Roger the miller beckoned him in with a hand as huge and red as a side of mutton. "May's well sit, m'lord, the thing's for you more than any of us."

Trelayne let himself down beside a thin, pimpled youth who glared his distaste. "Out with it, one of you."

He glanced from the miller to the weaver, who sighed and answered, "Derik's turned himself in for killing the guards."

"But he was nowhere near, and there's a witness!"

"What does it matter? They'd as soon string him up as go chasing after you," one of the other men put in. "My lord," he added, in exaggerated courtesy.

"Tell me all," he ordered, the dark patch on his face growing darker still with his anger. The thin scars of dragon's blood burned all over again.

"Seems he got there just after the guard. They's busy tossing Anmoria's, looking for you, or just for fun, I don't know," Roger said. "One o' them comes to Derik, to see what he knew, but I guess he'd taken it in already, and guessed what happened from what they said. Knocked the guard a good one, and made as if to run, but he knew he'd not get far. Made up some excuse why he came back to the scene, and they's happy enough to haul him off." He finished with a weary lifting of the hands, as if to say there was nothing to be done for it.

"We should never have run from the scene," Trelayne said, frowning.

"Don't talk nonsense," Anmoria said, and the other faces mirrored her astonishment.

"I killed those men defending you from rape. If we step forward and speak to that crime—"

"Ha!" a pudgy woman interjected. "Rape's a crime against a lay-dee—"she drew out the word, eyeing Anmoria, "and it wouldn't be the first time, eh, dearie?"

Anmoria flushed, finding reason to look anywhere but at Trelayne.

"Besides," a little man hurriedly put in, "what's the word of a peasant, and a woman at that. Any one of those men is worth five of us, far's they're concerned."

"There's still me," Trelayne insisted, balling his hand into a fist.

"You? And what's to trust about you, my lord?" the fat woman said. "You're the one as got him in all this trouble. Don't know why he'd risk his neck for a trumped-up dandy like you."

Her venom stung, taking him aback, and, as he looked around the faces, he saw how many of them agreed. Why indeed should Derik confess to save a nobleman who'd never done them a good turn? Only Roger the miller fidgeted under that gaze. He lifted his hands again, and let them flop to his broad lap, sending up a puff of the flour caught in his clothes.

"You're right, then, it concerns me more than any of you. I got him into it, in more ways than one," Trelayne said darkly.

"But," Anmoria started, laying a hand on his arm.

"It's true," he cut her off. "It's me he's to hang for. Gods know why."

"But what can you do?" Anmoria asked, more subdued.

"I'm a lord," he snapped, "what can't I do?" He glared at the peasants, who met his gaze sullenly, or with such disgust that it made him shudder.

Anmoria offered, "I'll testify, if you think it'll help."

Chilled, Trelayne shook his head. "You've already said they'd kill you for spite." When she looked about to protest, he added, "It wouldn't be the first time that's happened here, would it?"

Ducking her head, Anmoria didn't answer.

"So if it's not to be the laws of the court," said Trelayne slowly, considering the idea which had just come to him, "it must be the Code of Chivalry." The stillness of his face must have given them an glimpse into his mind, for Anmoria suddenly gripped his arm.

"What's that then?" the miller wondered aloud.

"The Code of Chivalry governs the ways of knights. When any man is sentenced to death, if a knight thinks it is unjust, he can stand for the condemned in single combat."

"So you'd fight a man t'prove the point?"

"Any man the magistrate names."

Squeezing his arm to gain his attention, Anmoria asked, "Could you win?"

The youth and the fat woman snickered, while several others rolled their eyes to the heavens.

"It depends on who's chosen, I guess," Trelayne said, shrinking from this flaw revealed in the scheme. Could he win? He'd killed a dragon, with a little help. He met Anmoria's gaze, and shivered in the light of it.

"If you want to impress the girl, that's done," crowed the fat woman, "but that still leaves us with what to do about Derik."

"The law won't help, and neither can we," someone's quiet voice observed.

The youth muttered, "Still don't see why we should," and received a swift elbow to the ribs from the man on his other side.

The gathering studied their feet in awkward silence.

Freeing himself from Anmoria's grip, Trelayne rose and shook off the blanket. "That only leaves me."

"If ye win, ye get his life," the miller said, still working it through, with a trembling of his double chins, "but if ye lose, ye both die, that right, m'lord?"

"No," Anmoria cried from behind him. She jumped up, grabbing his wrist. "Don't you see? Derik has already traded his life for you, he can't mean for you to refuse him."

"So I should let him die?" Trelayne held her with his eyes, his muscles quivering. "Whatever he means, whatever he thinks he's doing, the choice isn't his to make. I can't leave him, Anmoria, don't even ask it."

She met his gaze, unflinching, though her eyes beseeched him still.

"Stay here, safe," Trelayne commanded her. He pressed her hands together. Bending his head over them, he kissed her fingertips with delicate, desperate longing. Slowly, he drew their joined hands up toward the marvelous figure above, the unwinking eyes of the Blue Lady. Gazing at her beneath the temple of their arms, he whispered, "Pray for me."

Releasing her, Trelayne pounded up the stairs into the cool dawn light.

# CHAPTER

## FIVE

### *Fighting Fashion*

A STARTLED HOUSE GUARD ADMITTED Trelayne through the front gate, watching after him with his mouth hanging slightly open. A servant sweeping the stairs dropped his broom, and scrambled to collect it again, bowing to the master. Trelayne hurried by them, up to his own room. There, he surprised a manservant in the act of drawing the curtains.

"Good morning," the man squeaked.

From the rumpled condition of the bed, and of the man's own nightclothes, it was evident that he'd been sleeping in the master's bed. Following Trelayne's gaze, he reddened, pursing his lips, and letting out a little puff of air.

"Good to know you've been taking care of the place in my parents' absence," Trelayne remarked, throwing open a chest at the foot of the bed. "Sword polished too, I see."

He drew out the sword, lying wrapped in scabbard and belt. "I'll need my breastplate, and a bath—not in that order." He dropped the sword on his unmade bed, and pulled open a drawer.

Frowning, Trelayne looked up to find the man still goggling at him. "What is it?"

"Are you home then, my lord?" the manservant managed to inquire.

"For the moment. Get to it would you? I'm in a hurry."

"Yes, my lord, I can see that." He sketched a bow and left at a trot.

Requisitioning a basin full of water, Trelayne set himself to the careful task of shaving. He winced as he nicked himself, but stubbornly continued, schooling himself to patience. They'd not open the court until after breakfast, but he meant to be there, and every inch the gentleman.

When he'd finished his toilette, Trelayne hounded the servants out, and hunted through his clothes. He chose the things which Gwenyth had had no hand in—the deep blue shirt was none of her work, nor did his cream velvet doublet match anything of hers. Not the best choice for a battle, perhaps, but it couldn't be helped. The silken hose he found were much too fine as well, but all of his fighting clothes had vanished, carried off by well-meaning servants in anticipation of his settling down. Thus clad, he realized he had no boots. He had abandoned his own some time yesterday, letting his toes soak in the sunlight as he worked in Derik's yard. Had it been only yesterday? A pang of longing struck him, and he froze as if captured by magic.

The sun on his toes, the toss of Anmoria's hair, the simple joy of turning out his first proper spoke to make his friend's wheel: all of those things would be lost, if he lost. His mind returned to the wheel, the hub Derik had worked so carefully, the setting of the rim. Derik. His memory of sunlight cooled beside the dragon's fire. What good was the spoke without the wheel? As for Anmoria, he had killed three men to save her. Was Derik not worth one life, even if it must be his own?

Resolutely, Trelayne crossed his room, and strode to the end of the hall. Pausing but a moment, he pushed open his parents' richly carved doors. By the tall bed, mounded with down puffs and satin, he found what he was looking for: his father's sturdy winter boots, left behind in favor of something lighter. For Trelayne's purposes, they'd do. He sat on the bed to pull them on, and sank into the heap of feathers. Their cling annoyed him, and he fended them off, dropping instead to the hard floor. He jerked on the boots, and rose, catching the flash of movement. Trelayne took a step back and caught himself reflected in the full-length mirror by his mother's chest of furs.

His face and hands shone dark with sun, traced by the pale lines of scars. Blonde hair trailed over his shoulders, longer than it ever had been, framing the face. He stood in arrested motion, favoring his right leg. His shoulders, muscled from the month's labor, strained the silk of the shirt whose blue echoed that of his eyes. This was not the lithe dancer he had been. No longer the pale court-dweller who went out only in the shade of a carriage or an umbrella toted by a sweating servant. If the war had changed his heart and mind, his time among the peasants had forged his body. Trelayne clenched his fist. He would win this bout; he must win.

Trelayne bound back his hair with a ribbon of red, and tied the sash of his knighthood at his waist before he strapped on his sword.

In the stables, his war-horse greeted him with a whinny. "Saddle him," he told the groom, who scurried to obey.

Leading out the steed, the groom uttered a cry when he saw the sword at his master's side. "Where're you going, my lord? Hunting?"

"Hunting justice," Trelayne replied, swinging himself into the saddle without assistance.

The great horse longed to run after the weeks in stable, and Trelayne let him do it, thundering down the wide avenues, dodging a few early carriages and the odd merchant with a loaded wagon. They pranced to a halt outside the stone courthouse, and Trelayne slid down, rebuffing the man who came to take his stirrup. The sword raised eyebrows as his horse was lead to be stabled, and Trelayne knocked on the door to be admitted.

"I'm here," he announced to the guard on duty, "about Derik the wheelwright. I believe he's up today?"

"Yes, sir," the guard replied stoutly. "Wants only the magistrate's arrival to hang the bastard."

Through clamped teeth, Trelayne said, "We'll see about that. In the meantime, may I speak to the prisoner?"

"I, ah," the guard hesitated, shifting his pike from one hand to the other.

"Well?" Trelayne grinned down at the man. "Or shall I put you on report?"

"Ah, no, sir, I mean, that is," he fumbled with a keychain, "yes, sir."

"Excellent."

He followed the guard past several others, who offered him the salutes due a knight, and down stone steps to the dark underbelly of the court. The man ushered him through a gate of bars, and re-locked it behind them, leaving the keys with the guards outside. Trelayne nearly retched as the reek of sickness and human waste attacked his nostrils. Rows of prisoners to either side shrank back from the guard's boots, or came to the end of their chains to sneer at the man he escorted. More than one blob of spittle flew through the air and smacked against his clothes. Trelayne kept his gaze straight ahead, wondering how many of these others had committed no crime but that of being born poor. The dragonblood scars on his hands stung as he considered this, and he rubbed his hands together in a vain attempt to still the fire.

"On your feet!" the guard whacked one of the prisoners with the butt of his pike. "Gentleman to see you, Gods know why."

Derik heaved himself to his feet, swaying. He tilted his head to squint at Trelayne from eyes nearly swollen shut. The hitch in Derik's side showed plainly how the guards had handled him. Trelayne's scars threatened to tear themselves free and choke the guard of their own accord.

"Trelayne?" bloody lips gasped.

The guard's pike lashed out again, sharply cracking the prisoner's side. Derik fell against the wall. "My lord," he cried, correcting himself, "my lord." It came nearly as a whimper.

"That's enough," Trelayne snarled to the guard. He moved to the wall, searching the battered face. He reached out a hand to Derik's shoulder.

With something that might have been a smile, Derik raised his chained hands.

The guard's pike rammed forward, but Trelayne caught it with a jerk. He whirled to face the man still clinging to the other end. "I said that's enough." His voice smoldered with dragon fire, and the man backed away.

Trelayne released him, letting the guard amble up the line as if he'd meant to leave them anyhow.

Straightening himself as best he could, Derik had pushed off from the wall to stand on unsteady feet. "See you've got yourself up as a lord again," he muttered thickly. The relief that had earlier leapt in his eyes was gone, replaced by an impenetrable darkness.

"What're you doing here, Derik?"

"Thought I was saving your hide. What are you doing here?" He thrust out his chin to indicate the prison. He knotted his fingers together, letting his arms dangle to relieve the weight of the chain which ran to a thick loop in the wall.

"The same," Trelayne replied. "You don't deserve any of this."

"So what, will you break me free?" His derisive laughter was a pale shadow of the braying Trelayne had grown used to.

"I have a plan."

"No doubt." Derik's brows squeezed together. "Will ye get out, before it's you they chain to the wall."

"Why shouldn't it be me? It's my crime, Derik."

"For me, the charge is murder, and I'll be hanged; for you, they'd have said treason, Trelayne, I heard them. Should I have left you to it?"

He left unspoken the punishment for treason—the slow tearing of limbs from body. Derik silently watched the effect he'd had on his audience, the shudder that ran through Trelayne's body. "Better me than you, better—"

"Oh, I'm worth so much more, am I?" Trelayne spat back. "Five peasants to a lord, or so I've heard. What's that amount to, an arm?" He held up his right arm, the fingers splayed. "Or a leg, Derik. Don't you know I would give it if I could?"

The prisoner rested his head against the wall, letting his eyes slide shut. "I think you've just told me, my lord," he murmured so thickly that Trelayne strained to hear him.

"Magistrate's arrived!" one of the gate guards called.

The man in the aisle turned back to them. "Time's up, my lord."

Briefly, Trelayne grasped his friend's shoulder. "Forgive me what I do for you," he breathed.

"Aye, lord, if you'll do the same."

Before the guard had another excuse to clout Derik, Trelayne turned and hurried down the aisle. If they had been overheard, or if only his gesture had been recognized, Trelayne didn't know, but, as he passed, the prisoners flung no curses.

Upstairs, in the high courtroom, nobles had begun to convene. It had lately been the fashion to attend trials, especially those sure to end in execution. Such events lent a thrilling air to dinner conversation, or so Gwenyth had told him, a long time ago. He had accompanied her to the trial and death of a man accused of stealing a watch, a family treasure, the magistrate had been assured. Even then, Trelayne had grown a little sick at the sight of the man's face, told he would hang for the theft of a watch. Looking back, he felt surprised, and disappointed in himself, that he had thought to marry such a woman. Elegant she was, refined and educated, and colder than the grave. As he thought this last, his gaze wandered the court, seeking a bench.

Across the room, in the front row, he caught sight of Gwenyth's unmistakable curls, bobbing as she nodded to a companion. The heavyset man beside her had to be Sir Richard, the man who'd come calling before she cast her eyes on Trelayne. Sir Richard ran the city guard, and had taught the young Trelayne what he knew of swordplay, the gentleman's way, not the desperate tactics of man against demon. Once, the knight had been his idol, all that he could hope to be. Now, he lead the elite group of cutthroats and rapists they called the city guard. It turned Trelayne's stomach to recall his earlier admiration.

Gwenyth's head lifted, and Trelayne quickly ducked aside into the dark back row, standing in shadows to view the proceedings.

A trumpet sounded from the hall, and all turned to

watch the magistrate's slow progress, followed by two boys swinging incense to purify the court. Behind them came a phalanx of guards, standing aside to allow passage of the prosecutor and, after him, the prisoner.

By full light, his face resembled more a demon than a man. Chains bound his hands together, and linked a collar about his throat to the guards who chaperoned him. He walked hunched over, grunting in pain. The faces of the lords and ladies turned from him, all of those fine people revolted by the sight of him.

Though his scars twitched his hands, Trelayne did not turn from him, but kept his lone, kind gaze upon his pained progress.

Once, Derik's head turned, just a little, as if he could feel Trelayne's eyes, and Trelayne prayed this was true.

When the Magistrate had perched upon his high platform, arranging his black robes to his liking, the audience, too, resumed their benches. Many of them had brought embroidered cushions to keep them comfortable during the proceedings.

"Your honor," the prosecutor began, "this man stands accused of the vile slaying of three of our finest city guardsmen, men with wives and children at home, some of whom will speak today, if your Honor is willing."

The Magistrate graciously inclined his head, and the prosecutor went on, describing how the guards approached a house of ill-repute, and sought the woman who lived there. They had heard that she kept a secret stock of golden threads, the very threads reserved to royalty, and which she wove for common men. She denied it, of course, then offered to bribe the men with her body. When they refused, and would have arrested her, the whore ran into the street, screaming. Then it was that this man, her neighbor sprang from his house, with a sword in hand—another crime to add to his name. Without provocation, he flung himself upon the guards, quickly slaying the captain, and two others. Though grievously wounded—Trelayne grinned at this—one escaped, and went for reinforcements.

"That man?" the Magistrate clarified, pointing to the slumped figure of Derik. At that moment, he looked hardly capable of wielding a spoon.

"He's lately returned from war, your Honor," the prosecutor offered, then added, "where he claimed to have been fighting demons."

A ripple of laughter circulated in the stuffy room. Several of the ladies flapped their faces with fans of peacock feathers. As for Trelayne, his skin prickled with cold though his blood seemed to boil within him. Had it always been such a mockery, and he had simply been too innocent to see?

"Have you any witnesses?"

"Here, your Honor, is the man who escaped this brutal attack." He stretched out his hand, and a man in guard uniform rose unsteadily. His arm was in a sling, and his head bandaged, but he managed a brave salute.

Well he knew where the man had taken his blows, and none would be so pretty as that. Trelayne snarled. The people seated in front of him turned curious eyes, and Trelayne, too, looked around, pretending to be mystified.

"Does the prosecutor's account sound fair to you, my good man?"

The guard nodded stiffly—shouldn't that hurt his bandaged head, Trelayne wondered—"Aye, your Honor, he speaks the truth, though he might have cleaned it up some, for the ladies."

The Magistrate nodded sympathetically. "Thank you for leaving your bed to come to us. I'm sure your captain will reward your bravery."

The man bowed, and resumed his place to enjoy the show he'd helped create.

"Shall I ask the wives, your Honor?" the prosecutor offered. "Or the deprived children of these dead fathers?"

"Let them grieve in peace, sir, I think we've heard enough." He turned his formidable frown upon the prisoner. "Well, have you any defense?"

Derik pulled himself up straight, held up his chin above the iron collar. "What can I say, your Honor, to defend myself from such a charge?"

The audience let out a collective gasp. Such effrontery! How delicious, the ladies were murmuring behind their fans.

"Then I will." Trelayne's voice rang out from the back row. He reached the aisle in three long, sure strides. Stronger every day. The grin he wore held little mirth, but may have seemed as the demon's grin, full of teeth.

# CHAPTER
# SIX

### Right of Arms

"AND WHO MAY YOU BE, sir?" the Magistrate asked politely. The scribe dipped his pen in the ink, and waited on Trelayne's reply.

"Trelayne of Oak Hollow, son of Marshall, the lord of Drachmare, and Imogene his wife; Knight of the realm and veteran of the Demon War." His words echoed in the hall, especially these last, and stopped the titters in the ladies' throats, and stopped the smiles on the men's faces.

"Indeed," the Magistrate replied, his face losing some of that air of interest.

"I am here to stand for Derik the wheelwright, who fought beside me in that war. Who slew demons with me, and brought down their general with his own hand." His right hand clenched into a fist, scars writhing, and he spared a glance for Derik. His friend had grown, if such were possible. His breath shuddered in his chest, but his lips trembled into a smile. His eyes opened full, and fierce, glistening as he heard.

In the front row, Gwenyth sat frozen, her fan partially lifted, her lips in a queer half-smile, as if she were about to be sick.

"Your Honor, I say to you that this man, my companion in arms, would sooner give up his own life than to see another lose his life unjustly." Trelayne treaded carefully by the truth. "I declare before yourself, all the nobles here assembled, and every god in heaven or in earth that Derik has committed no crime."

The Magistrate shifted a touch uncomfortably. "What evidence have you to present, Sir Trelayne?"

"Here is my evidence," Trelayne cried, and drew his sword. In both hands, he held the blade hilt up, showing where the king's own seal gleamed with gold around a knight's sapphire. Holding the sword vertically before him, Trelayne turned a slow circle, so that none missed his intention. Over the pommel, his eyes met Gwenyth's and she shivered, leaning forward. Her pale breasts heaved in the low neckline, and her tongue darted to her lips.

Through his fervor, some little part of Trelayne, still vulnerable, quaked beneath that lusty gaze. Now, of all times, Gwenyth's body yearned for him.

Beside her, Sir Richard stiffened, eyes narrowed.

Swiftly, Trelayne turned back to the Magistrate.

"You seek the right of combat for this man's life?"

"I do."

The Magistrate rose to his hidden feet. "This is, ah, a most unexpected event, Sir Trelayne, and we, ah, have not prepared for such a duel—"

"I have, your Honor," a deep voice cut in. Sir Richard stood, his chest puffed out in its confection of bows and embroidery. Gwenyth's work. "I'll stand against him for the lives of my men, whose blood has already been spilt."

Trelayne dared not let his eyes drop from the weight of Richard's regard. Heavy-lidded eyes matched his, glittering from above the pointed beard.

"And you will be ready. . .?" the Magistrate quavered, once again out of his depth.

"Now." Trelayne formed the single syllable with every fiber of his being. If he delayed this too long, his courage might flag beneath the threat of Richard's sword.

As if sensing the thought, Richard smiled slightly. "I'd like an hour, your Honor, if that suits the claimant." He bowed his graying head toward Trelayne with easy grace.

"An hour, then, at the gallows field."

Trelayne shot a horrified glance to Derik, who sucked in a deep breath and let it out slow, eyes cast toward the heavens.

The trumpet blew, and the audience rose, witnessing the Magistrate's stately withdraw. Once the procession had passed by in reverse, the whispering began in earnest. Trelayne waited his turn to descend the narrow stairs, hearing his name on every breeze. Behind their fans, the ladies were studying him, and smiling at what they saw, while their escorts puffed and grunted, hurrying them along with firm hands under dainty elbows.

At last, he gained the open air, letting out a breath, letting go the steel he held inside. He trembled, facing the interminable hour. Outside, a different crowd gathered. Rough men and women, clad in dull grays and browns, with dark-eyed children to hand. Many of them had settled on the cobbles, despite the best efforts of the guard to move them along. This once, they would not be moved.

Roger pushed his way through the crowd, waving his enormous hands.

As if seeing Trelayne for the first time, the peasants fell silent, many rose, and bowed, then stood awkwardly, arms limp without their labor, waiting for what, he did not know.

"My lord, I beg you," the miller called as Trelayne hovered on the last step. "What news, my lord?" He bent his thick waist in a bow as low as he could manage.

"There will be a duel," he called to the crowd in a pale imitation of his earlier announcement. Suddenly, the weariness of the sleepless night caught hold of him. "I will fight Sir Richard, Knight of the City Guard, at the gallows in an hour's time. If I win," he drew a breath to sustain him, "if I win, Derik lives."

Some met this with a ragged cheer that died beneath the menacing stares of the guards around them. Those standing bowed again, or drifted off, and, as quietly as they'd waited, the crowd dispersed.

At Trelayne's side, Roger stood watching them go. He turned up his ruddy face. "Anmoria wants—"

"Don't let her come," Trelayne beseeched, gripping the miller's vast forearm.

"No fears, m'lord, the priestess'll handle her. No, I came for this." He fumbled beneath his work apron and brought out a scrap of cloth. The wool was dyed like fire, and shot with strands of gold. "She says a lady sends a kerchief when a knight's to battle, but, as she's got no kerchiefs, well, here's this."

Trelayne rubbed his fingers on the fabric, feeling in it Anmoria's warmth, and the tenderness of her embrace. "Tell her I will carry it by my heart."

Embarrassed, the miller turned up his hands, and gave a ghostly grin. "How's he look?"

"He's keeping his spirits up," Trelayne said, taking the excuse to tuck Anmoria's offering into his shirt. In fact, Derik looked like death already, like a man waiting to die.

The hour passed in restless walking the city streets. Trelayne's feet lead him down the paths of his childhood, through his own garden, down the little alley to Derik's house, and even to the Lion's Den. Nowhere did he stop, and no one did he greet, but watched the steady pace his feet kept, until, at last, they lead him to the north of town, to the barren place where the gallows stood.

On the low mound, black-clad men were wrapping a rope, testing the drop for Derik's weight. Shivering, Trelayne turned away. In the field below, benches and blankets spread out. The Magistrate's high seat had been set out, with an awning of cloth to keep the sun from his head. Beneath the shade of a spreading oak, the finest of the lords arrayed themselves with padded seats and servants to pour the wine. Viceroy Brisson, who hadn't bothered with the trial, relaxed on a portable sofa, tended by his personal squadron of servants. Nearby, a company of musicians plucked out delicate melodies for the ladies' delight as they sat stitching their flowers. On the far side of that tree, Sir Richard's pavilion had been raised. His squires bustled about, on errands far too grand for the gallows field.

The brown and common folk sat in the sun, some on leather hides, and some on the bare earth they knew so well. They had brought neither amusements nor music, but waited, silent, except to hush the children too young to be left home. Their dark eyes watched his approach, but Trelayne hesitated. Lacking pavilion, or servants, he did not know where to wait out his doom.

Suddenly, a hand plucked at his sleeve, and he turned to find Gwenyth's cool gaze upon him. Wearing a different dress for the occasion, she sipped a tall goblet which smelled of sweetness. "Good day, Sir Trelayne. Perhaps you'd care for a drink?"

"Thank you, no," he replied stiffly, then, "my lady," an afterthought. He chuckled to himself; his manners had faded so quickly.

Gwenyth's face formed a pretty pout. "You would not be laughing at me, for some reason?" The petulance in her voice hinted at her interest, and Trelayne glanced away from her.

"Why should I laugh at you?" His wandering eyes fell upon the ragged crowd of peasants as more of them gathered, their faces bleak.

She clucked her tongue to call back his eyes. "If Richard wins, I think I'll let him marry me."

"As well you should, Gwen. He is the prize that you deserve."

Lifting her chin, she replied, "Of course there is the matter of the contract our parents signed—oh!" She pressed a hand to her mouth, eyes wide in mock surprise. "But if he wins, you die, Trelayne, is that not so? Pardon my blunder in mentioning it."

Beneath the leather gloves he wore, Trelayne's scars flared to life. "Naturally, if you'll forgive me for missing the wedding."

"Naturally," she murmured, unsure what he was getting at.

"I'll be sorry not to see it, though," he paused, then smiled almost wistfully. "I've never witnessed a demon bride."

Her rouged lips twisted tight, her fingers on the goblet stem threatening to snap it in two. "May the best man win." Gwenyth turned her back to retreat across the field where her latest beau prepared for battle.

By the rules of chivalry, the combatants should be in like gear, and similarly weaponed. Still, Richard had laid out the full array of his weaponry, from heavy mace to sharp lance, a visual boast meant to demoralize his enemy. Trelayne hated to admit that it was working.

Clad in a golden breastplate, Richard was bending and stretching with his sword, swinging it in practice arcs about his head, and bringing it down on invisible enemies. An admiring crowd watched him work. Gwenyth appeared among them, clapping in girlish glee at his every stroke.

Trelayne turned away, finding himself again faced with

the peasants. One or two of the whores among them blew kisses, which he received with awkward smiles. More than one lady on the other side had done the same, ladies who'd never given him a second glance before. Somehow, these seemed more genuine; not just a tease, but an advertisement of their willingness. A peasant whore, Anmoria had called herself. He pressed a hand to his chest, where her favor hid against his skin. He pictured her, for just a moment, in Gwenyth's gown, with its tight bodice, low neck, and skirts to sweep the floor. Anmoria could be a princess, he decided, a princess with the heart to match.

Roger the miller came up the slope, and bowed. "Gods be with ye," he called out before dropping his bulk to the ground.

The trumpet sounded through the sultry air, and Trelayne turned to watch the Magistrate's entrance, with his entourage of scribes, guards and executioners. Among them, Derik held his head high, a hitch in his step the only sign that every movement touched a nerve. Crossing the field, he raised up his chained hands, palms together. From a distance, the gesture was for victory, for life. Now, Trelayne could also see the prayer in it, for the Blue Lady's compassion, whichever way it fell.

Richard emerged from his shade, gleaming, cool, and easy on his feet. Trelayne, too, moved toward the field. Slipping his sword in and out to test its readiness, and his own, he pushed aside his boyhood adulation, and studied Richard through the eyes of war.

The older man had gained a soft belly since their

lessons. His girth even spread the plates which guarded his heart, creating a wider gap at the side, as if he'd not been in armor for some time now. A less confident man would have borrowed better-fitting plate. Determined this would not shake him, Trelayne continued his survey. Though Richard's swings were well-executed, they were slow, exhibition style. It might carry over to the bout enough to give Trelayne an edge. The dragonblood scars wormed upon his skin, lending a curious swiftness to his fingers as they drummed upon his thigh. Trelayne's heart stopped pounding in his chest, and he let his lop-sided smile take command. If he was not the man he'd been, nor was Richard, and the time had gone to his own advantage.

"We meet here to try, by test of arms, the life of this prisoner, Derik the wheelwright." The Magistrate gestured toward the kneeling figure. Across the field, their eyes met, and Trelayne grinned. "The duel," continued the Magistrate, "will be with sword only, and to the death."

A cheer rose from the courtly lords, waving their goblets in wild salute. Richard inclined his head to them, and winked to Gwenyth beneath her ribboned parasol.

"Gentlemen, greet your brother in arms. May the gods provide us a champion of truth this day."

Richard and Trelayne met at the center, gripping right hands to right shoulders, the knightly salute. They smiled into each other's eyes, their hands firm, proving strength, but careful neither to reveal, nor to probe, too much. Gwenyth's yellow favor hung at Richard's sash, fluttering its flowers as the two parted. They drew their swords and held them erect, points to the sky.

Once more, the trumpet blew.

Two swords slashed down, completing the salute as their bearers slipped into fighting stance. They circled restlessly, eyes darting for any sign of attack. Richard's sword danced and wove through the air, trying to draw Trelayne's eye, and failing.

Instead, Trelayne focused on his opponent's balance, how he swayed from foot to foot, and caught the moment when he feinted right. His own blade flashed up, caught and parried in a chime of steel.

Again, circling.

Richard blew out a breath through his nostrils, and sprang for it. No feint this time, no casual gauge, he drove into Trelayne's defense.

Flinching at the suddenness of the attack, still Trelayne did not drop his vigilance for a second. He slipped aside, and traded blows in a crashing of steel. Then fell away, ducking, coming around from the side.

Richard spun to meet him, and Trelayne's well-placed blade scraped across the golden breastplate, carving a line into the base metal below.

A muscle in Richard's jaw leapt at the sound.

Trelayne pressed the advantage, raining blows upon him until their swords rang. The dragonblood seemed to swirl and move on his hands, urging him to the kill.

His blade slid along Richard's and snicked a sliver of red from the man's cheek.

Richard's fighting smile became a grimace as he bore

down, battering, but gaining little ground.

A backhand slid by Trelayne's defense, but smacked flat against his shoulder. A hard blow, which he rolled out from under.

The sword flashed over his head, and Trelayne drove upward. His blade this time caught flesh, gashing Richard's left arm from elbow to wrist in a bloody line.

Richard cursed, the jaw-muscle leaping beneath his skin.

Trelayne laughed aloud, swiftly parrying a clumsy response.

Furiously, Richard retreated, struggling to maintain control as Trelayne forced him to give ground.

Trelayne reveled in the chase, careful not to over-extend himself. Let Sir Richard have a little rest. He was beaten, and the flickering of his eyes showed he knew it, too.

Then from the crowd, a voice rose above the shouting. "Richard, the knee! His right knee!"

The voice caught him off guard, even more than the blow. Gwenyth's voice, her face contorted with the fury of the fight. Gasping, Trelayne tried to spin away. Inside, he was already reeling when the slash hit home.

Richard's blade tore into his flesh, carving through tendon and muscle, chinked into bone, and tore free again, flinging him aside with its power.

Trelayne rolled, his sword beneath him. He curled a moment into himself, came to rest, and pushed himself to his knees, hands fumbling blindly for the blade.

Dirt stung his eyes, and blood dampened his lips. His ears rang with her voice, over and over. From the rend in his flesh, arrows of pain shot through him. His mouth hung open in a silent scream, for no sound he made could free him from this agony. His heart and lungs cried for space to beat, to breathe, as he gulped at the air. Dully, he knew he must move, mustn't crouch there on the ground, waiting to die.

Cutting through the ringing of his ears, he caught the cheering of the lords, the triumphal shouts echoing from the gallows hill. On the other side, someone called his name.

Shaking his head, desperate to clear a space for him to think, Trelayne at last found his sword. He clenched it both hands, dragged up the immense weight of it, and raised his head.

The shadow that was his opponent loomed into focus. Richard stood a few feet away, but did not strike the killing blow. He panted, patting his sweat-streaked brow. Noticing Trelayne's impotent gaze, Richard's expression turned grim. He drew a little nearer, but still did not raise the sword which dangled in his grasp. "You have fought well, Sir Trelayne," Richard said, his voice betraying his surprise. "If you will plant your sword and yield to me, you may walk from the field, Trelayne. I will grant your life."

Every muscle shrieked and quivered. Trelayne struggled to make them work, to understand what the man wanted, the man towering over him. Hadn't it been a dragon? He was so sure.

His eyes searched the sidelines, saw the faces of the lords arrayed against him, but half-bent, their drinks forgotten. The ladies dabbed their eyes and sighed to one another, shaking their heads, and Gwenyth. . . after so much, still her blow tore at his heart.

Trelayne got his sword by the hilt, and made a swipe as if to jab it into the ground. He missed. Laughing without sound, Trelayne shook his head again. How could he miss such a target? Gods, how Derik would laugh for that.

Through the haze of dust which rose above the field, he found the place where Derik, like him, knelt at the side of an armed man. His eyes squinted to seek out Trelayne's, his chained hands dangled to heavy to hold, but his chin thrust up, and his lips worked. Listening intently, Trelayne brought the words into focus, ". . .you slew the dragon, Trelayne; you fought the demons, now get up. . ." Over and over, like a meditation, or a prayer.

Trelayne swung his sword again, and struck the dirt, the sword sticking there, and wavering in his grip. A great cheer rose from the lords, and a grunt of satisfaction from Richard. Somewhere far off, a few peasants moaned, a few dirty children wept.

Derik's lips stilled. His shoulders sagged, and the chain bore his head to the ground.

# CHAPTER

---

## SEVEN

### *The End of Sorrow*

THE DRAGONBLOOD GONE SILENT AT last, Trelayne shifted his grip on the sword. He turned his face back to the enemy. Richard stood poised to accept his hand in surrendering the field.

Trelayne edged his good leg under him. Using the sword as a steel cane, he dragged himself up from the dirt, inch by terrible inch. The lords groaned, but the peasants' whoops of joy swept every other sound away. Leaning on his sword, gritting his teeth, Trelayne stood.

The peasants surged to their feet along with him, crying his name.

Gently, Richard shook his head, and raised his sword.

Trelayne turned his body, letting the right leg bear a little strain, trying to ignore the pulsing blood spattering from within. "Have at you," he whispered through blood and grit, "I will not yield."

Richard came for the leg again, as Trelayne knew he would. He gathered himself, waiting the eternity it took for the blade to fall. Richard came for the leg, and Trelayne let him have it. Even as Richard's wild swing carried him by, Trelayne's blade ripped from the ground.

Steel cut a perfect arc in the dust, and smashed into Richard's side where the plates gapped open, tearing up from belly to sash to snap the ribs like so many strands of wool. Trelayne finished with his blade held high, his opponent rolling into the dust, eyes and mouth gaping a final astonishment.

Trelayne's sword arm fell, the blade again point down, bearing his weight. "The point is proved, your Honor," he said, meeting the Magistrate's harsh gaze.

Silence echoed from the right, while the peasants danced about each other, hollering to the Lady.

"Indeed, the man's life is won."

Derik shook his fists in the air, his bray of laughter winging through to Trelayne's ears.

"Take him away," the Magistrate said, motioning for the guards.

"I won his life," Trelayne howled, and the peasant's rejoicing died away.

Rising from his chair to be assisted down, the Magistrate offered a wan smile. "His life indeed, sir, but not his freedom. Take him away."

A guard jerked on Derik's chain, easily toppling the

stunned prisoner.

Trelayne's legs crumpled beneath him, the right foot turning inward with a sickening crack, and he plunged face first to the dirt, his upthrust sword gently swaying in his wake, firmly planted.

As Trelayne lay in a heap, beating the ground with a helpless fist, a roar of rage built among the peasants. City guards sprang to life, brandishing pikes and swords.

In the confusion, Derik broke from his own guards, sprinting, shouting. "Trelayne!" he cried at the top of his lungs. "Trelayne!"

Someone laid hold of the chain, and hauled him back, so that his last words sputtered, "We live, Trelayne!" Hurriedly, they bundled him off to some yet darker prison.

Dirt filled his mouth and nostrils, so that his lungs fought for breath, but Trelayne did not heed them. Fury and anguish tore through him in equal measure. Through the slit of one eye, he saw Sir Richard's squires bending over their master's body, draping him with velvet. Still, his mouth gaped blood, and his eyes held their stunned expression. Grunting with the effort, the squires bore the loser from the field, while the victor lay gripped in his despair. A wail rose in him, as the Magistrate stepped down and fled the scene, but the sound died before reaching his lips. No sound could do justice to the depth of his pain.

Soft voices fluttered down around him through the fog, the cultured whispers of lords and ladies, fascinated, afraid to come near, but afraid to miss a minute.

"Mother of Sorrows! Get away, curse ye!" a man bellowed,

shoving through the on-lookers with little regard to wealth or gender. A hand like raw meat descended as the miller threw himself down in the dirt. He swept the tangle of hair from Trelayne's face, and stared into the revealed eye. "What can I do? What can I do?" he mumbled, quickly taking in the blood, and the dreadful twist of the downed man's foot.

Roger stripped off his apron and slipped it around the gaping wound.

"Come away, you," a new voice commanded, "We'll see to him, there's a doctor on the way."

"The devil you will!" Roger shot back. "Will his blood stain your hands?" He bound the cloth as tightly as he dared, stemming the flood, then leaned close to Trelayne. "Sorry," he whispered, sliding the sash from Trelayne's waist. Above the knee, he pulled tight a tourniquet. He pulled free the straps of the breastplate and flung it aside. "I'll get you," he said, placing a careful hand under Trelayne's shoulders.

"The doctor's on the way, I tell you," one of the lords repeated. He waved for some assistance from the beleaguered guards. "Someone remove that man."

Even as he said it, a tall man cut through the company followed by a retinue of assistants carrying medical equipment. The last man held a gleaming saw.

"Doctor!" a liveried servant ran up, sparing a brief glance for Trelayne. "Doctor, the viceroy's taken ill."

The doctor considered Roger's makeshift bandage, and said, "I'll see to the viceroy and return. Keep still," he advised. "Try not to aggravate the injury." He went quickly back out of the circle, with his little procession following.

"Will ye stay?" Roger asked, his face filling Trelayne's vision.

A sharp shake of the head. "What've they done for me?" he muttered.

"Aye, sir. I'll get ye," he repeated, but was answered by another shake.

"I'll not be carried." He moved his hands under him, heaving himself up with the miller's firm support. "I won this field, whatever they do." He wiped the dirt from his face, pushing back his hair. "I'll not be carried from it like the dead."

"Ye're a fool," Roger told him plain, but adjusted his grip, and together, they rose.

The knot of lords gasped, pulling a little back.

"Out of the way," the miller shouted, and the crowd parted, opening a corridor to the restless peasantry, contained in a perimeter of armed men.

A cry arose, callused hands waving their exultation. The crowd broke, shoving themselves through to gather before him. One small boy darted past, and returned, shaking and cautious, with Trelayne's bloody sword borne across his palms.

Miller and knight shared a grim glance. Trelayne tightened his hand on Roger's shoulder, and they moved forward, Roger taking the weight. Grins, and even tears, sparked the faces of the peasants. A woman thrust him a handful of lilies plucked from some lady's garden. Another draped his brow with ivy, and a man hung a pendant of the Blue Lady about his neck. Each stepped forward quickly, shyly, their eyes still cast down, and was quick again to clear his path.

When they had painstakingly walked past the last of the peasants, the ranks closed behind. Muttering city guards, sensing that the danger had passed, lowered their weapons, drawing warily back.

With a parade of laborers and shopkeepers, his sword carried by a child whose only garment was a grubby tunic, Trelayne had his triumphal march. They matched his pace in its hesitation, their voices falling silent. No banners waved, nor trumpets sounded as the victor left his field behind, headed not for the feast of celebration, nor the comforts of down and satin, but for the dark houses and dried mutton of the peasants' quarter. Trelayne held his head high, admitting of neither pain nor betrayal. One hand dug into Roger's thick shoulder, the other strangled the bouquet of lilies. If he had been the one carried from the field, the flowers would have decked his grave.

Down the hill they traveled, leaving behind the gallows' shadow, until they reached the cobbled street. Trelayne stumbled, his head pitched forward, and Roger gathered him to his chest. Lifting the young man in his immense arms, Roger set off at a lumbering run.

The miller bellowed, "To Derik's place, fetch the healers!" Others hurried to do his bidding.

By the time Roger arrived with his burden, the house was open, the healers waiting. Children hauled buckets of water from the well, while their mothers tore strips from their linen sleeves, making ready.

They lay Trelayne on the table, cutting through the bloodied hose and apron both, jerking free his father's boot. The healers examined the ruin of his leg, the unnatural twist of his calf. They probed his knee, splashing water over the flesh, sending a river of red, flecked with chips of bone, to wash over the floor. The three of them shared a sigh, and long look.

"Hold him," said one of the men.

Understanding, Roger knelt and wrapped his arms around Trelayne, taking his head upon one broad shoulder. Firm hands clasped above his ankle, and wrenched. The bones shrieked pain up his thigh, and he struggled in the miller's grasp, but collapsed, screaming. Roger grimaced, but did not relax.

They worked more slowly now, cleaning the wounds with a steady stream of cloth from the women's skirts and sleeves. The crowd at the door parted, letting Granny Falcon pass, and with her ran Anmoria, her bruised face streaked with tears. She crouched at Roger's shoulder, stroking Trelayne's brow, pressing her cheek to his when the healers started their binding, first smearing his skin with healing herbs.

When they stepped away, Granny creaked to his side. She raised herself on tip-toes to peer down at him with blind eyes, with her jagged, reassuring smile. She held her gnarled hands first to his face, then ran them the length of his body, and back up to the new binding at his knee. Here she started crooning, that marvelous trill of sound which seemed to draw away his pain. His torn muscles twitched and pulled, struggling to begin healing the rends. Warmth tingled in

# Elaine Isaak

both directions and, when she withdrew, Trelayne let out a long breath, took in another without shuddering.

Roger at last eased his hold, letting Anmoria's slender arms sneak in for a moment.

Trelayne turned his face to hers, blinking back tears.

Smiling bravely, she let hers flow.

Touching her face with gentle fingers, he whispered, "We live."

She nodded, and did not answer.

He drank a dipper of water, topped with herbs to make him sleep, and was carried to the cushioned alcove.

Derik's mother moved her head up and down on her wrinkled neck, watching him settled into her bed. Through her crooked teeth, she mumbled, "Bless you, my lord," and retreated.

With Anmoria laying damp cloths on his forehead, Trelayne drifted into sleep, and did not dream.

From time to time, darkness gave way to dim light, to vague faces bending over him, or soups and medicines being poured down his throat. Somebody washed him, carried off the straw cushions and laid down new ones while careful arms supported him. Several times he drifted up into the cloud of the old woman's singing, her hands draped gently over the wound. A steady murmur of voices kept him company, Anmoria's and the miller's, and the whispering of children, or the gruffness of their fathers. Once or twice, he roused to a meeting of some sort, heated voices, quickly stilled at his slightest movement.

Ages passed in stillness by the time he opened his eyes,

and blinked away sleep. A warm body huddled against his side, chest rising and falling in the ancient rhythm. Trelayne's head was clear, unfogged, for once, by potions and herbs, blessedly free from pain, if only for the moment. A single lantern, turned low, provided the glow. He moved carefully, raising a hand from the wool blanket, cautiously feeling the sleeper's face.

Anmoria's chin nudged into his touch, and a murmur of pleasure rose in her throat, then her eyes popped open in the gloom. "Trelayne," she whispered, starting to sit up.

He stopped her with his hand on her hair. "Stay, please stay."

Nestling down again, she asked, "How do you feel?"

"Tired," was the immediate response. "I can feel the throb, but it doesn't hurt, not yet."

"It will again," she sighed. "I'm sorry."

He nodded into the pillow. "How long have I been sleeping?"

"A fortnight."

"What?" The surprise jolted his exhaustion from his mind.

"Granny and the healers," Anmoria supplied. "All of those soups I fed you had something in them."

"Of course it was you," he murmured to himself, remembering now the softness of the arms supporting him, the coaxing voice. "I think it worked, whatever it was."

"And the singing. What I'd do to learn to sing like she does," Anmoria sighed into his chest. Her fingers circled in the fine, blond hair above his heart. "I should let you sleep," she said. "I'm not supposed to be here, like this."

"Tell me about the Blue Lady," he said quickly, before she could move.

"Very well." She smiled.

"When the gods were young," she began, "they argued all the time. At that time, they hadn't got their tasks yet, so each would try to do whatever came to mind. Sometimes, they all watched over ships at sea, and there was none keeping wolves from the sheep, or making sure the wheat grew tall. Since they constantly got in each other's way, they used to throw storms back and forth, and raise up mountains where the plains had been. Mortals cowered in fear, worried for themselves every moment, not knowing if the gods would watch over them, or if the next storm would blow them from their homes.

"There was a woman named Margaret, who lived by the coast, a fisherman's wife. When the gods watched the sea, her husband came home. When the gods cared for children, her sons grew strong. But the day came when one of those storms tossed her husband into the sea, and one of those mountains burst from the field her sons were tending, flinging them into the air, and Margaret tore her hair and wept for four nights and three days. On the last dawn, she rose up, determined that the gods should hear her grievance."

Anmoria laughed, her body quivering against him. "Being gods, they were not pleased to hear her out. Margaret climbed one of those mountains, and found Ishdren at the top. When she cursed her for the death of her children, the goddess cast her up into the sky, caring not where she fell.

But as she flew, Ishdren realized that she was right, and she took it as her duty to tend the fields.

"The blue of the sky tinged Margaret's head and shoulders, so that, when she fell back again, she did not look as other men. Next she rowed from the shore, in search of storms. At the eye of a hurricane, she found Falanel, and cursed him for the death of her husband. Furious, he threw her down into the sea, heedless of whether she drowned. Even as she sank, he understood her sorrow, and took upon himself to watch over the seas. The blue of the ocean stained Margaret's legs and body, so that, when she swam to shore, all of her was blue.

"She went from god to god, and spoke of her sorrow, and, one by one, they chose their places, patrons of women, shopkeepers, those lost, and those found. And as she traveled, they saw in her the guardian of the weak, who dared defend the frightened people even from the gods themselves."

Anmoria laid her palm flat, feeling Trelayne's heartbeat. "She is the one who listens for us, who carries our sorrow to the gods."

"And the lords forbade worshipping her."

Bitterly, she replied, "They do not hear us, why should they wish the gods to hear us? Why should they seek the end of our sorrow?"

A tremor ran through him, and Anmoria gasped. "Not you, Trelayne, of course I don't mean you."

"You have no cause to love the nobility." He snorted. "They dare call themselves noble. How can I say 'your Honor' to a man who is without it?"

"I haven't heard you talk this way before, Trelayne." She lifted her head, resting her chin on his chest to watch him.

"Winning the gallows field has shown me a whole new world in the place I thought I knew. The Code of Chivalry, the rule of law, justice, nobility, honor, mercy." He shook his head. "Before that day, I had been disappointed in my people. Until then, I had not been ashamed of them. Of us," he amended quietly.

Anmoria sat up, her palm pressed to his chest. "Don't say that, Trelayne, as if you were one of them, not after what you've done."

"Ha! Derik's alive—or he was when I saw him—but imprisoned, and you can be sure they'll do their damnedest to kill him. Great gods, if this is the way you've been treated all these years, I can't see why you've not revolted years ago. Or even two weeks ago."

"Because we were waiting for someone to lead us," Anmoria said simply, her face aglow from the lantern's flame. "We were waiting for you."

Trelayne started laughing, head thrown back, but, when she made no sound, he drew himself up to look at her. "You're serious."

"Aye, that I am, Trelayne. There's been talk—there's always talk, since I was a girl, but the next day there were sheep to tend, and blankets to weave, and we got so tired all over again. All that talk, and all you had to do was look around to see that nothing ever changes. Who are we, Trelayne? The small, the low, the stupid—"she placed her fingers on his lips for silence—"how do we overcome a thousand years of that. We're not strong enough, not brave enough, not good enough to take arms against the lords." She stopped for a breath, and smiled. "Until you, Trelayne, you and Derik."

"I don't understand."

"Two things we saw, at the gallows field. First, we saw that the Code of Chivalry is not all lies. You didn't need to fight, Trelayne, you could have run, or been still, and nobody would blame you."

With some trepidation, Trelayne asked, "And second?"

"You did it for us," she replied. "You showed us all that a lord should be, and lay down your life for a peasant. If he could stand against the dragon at your side, if he could be so bold to sacrifice for you, if he could be worthy of your life, Trelayne, then what's stopping us? Couldn't any of us be the hero?"

"I'd no idea," he breathed through her fingers.

"Wait'll you see them! Gerard, the boy who carried your sword, must've grown six inches that day. Every morning he comes to polish it, sitting at your feet. Roger's been served a round on the house for every night since then. The fields are full of the story of the Demon War. Oh, they wanted to go for Derik, and burn the Magistrate's house, and tear that bitch from her bed—"she broke off suddenly, her cheeks darkened. Her fingers slid from his face back into her lap.

"Gwenyth."

"Aye, Gwenyth." She bowed her head.

Trelayne frowned. Why hesitate to speak Gwenyth's fate? Then his pulse fluttered, and he tried to see beyond the veil of her hair. He dared a tremulous smile, and reached out to tuck her hair over her shoulder. "I loved her once, or thought

I did," he said, "but it was so long ago, I can't remember why."

Her eyes shone, and she covered her mouth.

"Anmoria," he sighed, unsure what to say. Her shoulder quivered beneath his hand, and a shudder ran through him.

"You shouldn't look that way at me," she whispered, turning away.

"Why not? If Derik is worthy of my life, Anmoria, why not you?"

"After what you've heard, what you've seen? I know there's talk, me being alone—those cursed guards and what they did—"

"Their fault, not yours," he murmured, "Never yours. What I've heard is your compassion, what I've seen is your spirit, Anmoria. You are the most beautiful woman I have ever known."

Her shoulders quaked as her head shook in mute denial.

"It's not about gowns and jewels and courtly airs. I've had those, and they betrayed me. But you—"

"I'd never betray you," she whispered fiercely.

"You're brave, and kind, and true in a way that Gwenyth never was, nor could she ever hope to be." He stroked her unkempt hair with trembling fingers. "Anmoria," he said, "I love you." For a long moment, they sat silent, and his heart stopped beating, to listen to her breath.

"I never thought to hear those words," she said, almost a moan. At last she turned, wiping the tears away. Then she smiled, and the tears flowed in spite of her, and Trelayne was kissing her eyes, her cheeks, her full, warm lips. He pulled her close, and held her tight, and the fire of her blazed through him until the pain, the fear, the darkness fell away in light.

# CHAPTER

---❧---

# EIGHT

### *To the Gate*

THE NEXT NIGHT BROUGHT COUNCIL as farmers, laborers and tradesmen crowded into Derik's tiny hut. Roger, with his new-earned status, presided, calling the eager gathering to order. Trelayne and Anmoria sat on the bed. For the occasion, she had made him a tunic of the flame-colored cloth, its illegal threads-of-gold gleaming in the lantern-light.

"We're ready, my—Trelayne—and we've set a watch," Roger said. "So what're we to do?"

"First things first, where's Derik, and how do we get him out?"

"They've got him on the gate," an urchin piped up. "I spotted him." He grinned up at Trelayne, who offered an encouraging smile to the little spy.

"Which gate?" he prompted.

Several of the men exchanged black looks. "The lower gate of the citadel, sir. Where they bring the prisoners."

"On gate means he's got to turn the wheel that raises and lowers it," Anmoria supplied.

"A dozen times a day, or more. That heavy bloody thing," another man said, rolling his shoulders as if he knew. "Most can't take it even this long."

"They want him dead," Roger agreed, "but he's not having it." He grinned. "Waitin' fer you, he is, like us."

"Let me think." Trelayne took a swallow of water from a waiting mug. The citadel gate—on the one hand, they had the ideal inside man, if they got his attention before that of the guards, on the other hand, the lower citadel teemed with fighting men, better trained and better armed. And the upper level—"How about the Viceroy," Trelayne mused aloud.

"Don't you know?" someone asked.

"Course he don't," another scoffed, "he's been here since it happened, hasn't he?"

Roger rapped on the table for order. "Viceroy's dead. The day of the Gallows Field, his heart gave out at the battle. That cursed doctor went to see, but he knocked off already."

"Blast! I was hoping to use the Viceroy's Ball," Trelayne muttered.

"Oh, that's on, all right. Must have their fun, mustn't they? The burghers've sent for a new viceroy, but the king's sent no word."

"Still mopping up the war, no doubt. How about the new captain of the guard?"

"A skinny git by the name of Cragan," a woman replied, she winked. "Not much there, you don't mind my saying."

Trelayne blinked at her. "You've been to see him?"

"Oh, aye. We've not just waited for ye, sir, we've laid some plans of our own. Kept an eye out haven't we?" She laughed, and the sound was echoed by the others.

"Trouble is, there's so many of them, specially there, and not so many of us able to fight."

"We'll need a diversion to bring them out, without dividing our number," Trelayne observed.

Anmoria, noticing the plural, nodded her agreement.

"Can we be ready for the Ball?"

"Six days, now," Roger murmured. "Aye, I think we can. As Maggie said, we've not been idle. Making weapons, watching the guards, much as they've watched us."

"So, an army to hide near the gate, and Derik inside to be sure the gate doesn't close. Let the first wave of guards go by, then in you go. Get hold of their armory, and we're ready to take them on."

"Simple," Anmoria said, "but what's to make the guards leave?"

"We'll go to the ball," he replied. "I'll show up on the viceroy's doorstep with two dozen of our finest whores, pickpockets and stable cleaners. They'll be so riled up, they hardly see straight. Trelayne the madman inviting his friends to the ball." He raised his mug to them, and was rewarded with cheers and clapping.

Anmoria frowned. "You're making yourself the bait to the trap. I don't like it."

He took her hand in his. "Who better?" he asked gently. "They can't deny me, they can't admit me. Besides—" he flashed a feral grin—"I want to see their faces."

"Me, too," she said, unsmiling.

"You're not to come," he replied firmly. "I don't want you hurt."

"We are in this together," Anmoria told him, with a gesture that took in the room, "all of us."

Giving in, he smiled. "There's no one I'd rather have beside me at the ball."

"Settled then," Roger said gruffly, fidgeting on his perch on the table. "Only one other thing." He waved a hand, and a small, dark man came forward. In his hands, he held a crutch carved of maple, with swirling patterns of dragons the length of it.

"For the dragon slayer," he mumbled, holding it out.

Trelayne ran his hand along the fine carvings. "You made this? It's beautiful."

"Secret to it," the carver said. He took hold of the armrest at the top, and gave it a twist. From the center, a shaft of darker wood rose up. He tilted it to offer it to Trelayne.

Grasping the handle, Trelayne slid forth a slender blade as long as his arm, gleaming and wickedly pointed. He turned it in the air before him, seeing how it caught the light. He slipped the blade home again, and turned the armrest back into place. "Remarkable! How can I thank you?"

"Her idea," the little man replied, drifting back into the audience.

Anmoria shrugged. "A man's got to get around, and you

can't very well wear a sword to the ball, can you?"

"Indeed I cannot." He swept up her hand, and kissed the back of it, receiving a chorus of catcalls from the others.

The next six days passed in a flurry of activity for the makeshift army, and frustrating lethargy for their chosen general. Adjusting to using the crutch, Trelayne paced the house, then the street, and finally was able to go to the blacksmiths to cast an approving eye over their stealthy work. Long knives and hatchets honed to razor's edge found their way into packs and under cloaks. They never forged anything so obvious as a sword, but still the weapons flowed. The city guards patrolled in small troops, never so few as four, and Trelayne nodded to them coolly when they passed, then grinned behind their backs.

At last, the evening came. Trelayne found himself dressing with more help than he'd ever had before as Granny and Derik's mother fussed over him, with the help of a few of the children. The women and men of his distractionary force wore their best wools and linens, scrubbed and proud. When the door opened, and Trelayne stepped out, leaning on his magnificent crutch, many bowed or curtseyed, and Trelayne shook his head, laughing.

"Enough of that, now," he told them. "For tonight, you are all lords and ladies. Are you ready?"

"Aye!" they shouted, and their skirts and coats clinked with hidden daggers.

"Sir?" a little voice asked, and Trelayne looked down to find Gerard, his young sword-bearer, looking up at him with worried eyes, the sword held out on both palms. "What about this, sir?"

Trelayne lowered himself stiffly to the boy's level. His leg had healed much faster than he'd expected, but it was not whole, nor would it ever bend as once it had. "Gerard, I can't wear my sword to the ball," he explained gently. "I thought you knew that."

Tears gathered in the boy's eyes, and his chin quivered as he tried to master himself. Trelayne set a careful hand upon his shoulder, meeting the watery gaze.

"There is something you can do for me, but you'll need to be very brave, and very careful."

The boy nodded eagerly. "I can be! I am!"

"You know where Derik is kept, you've carried the messages."

Another nod.

"Wrap up this sword so that nobody knows what it is, and bring it to where the army is hiding. Give it to Derik when his chains are struck free. Tell him that this is the sword that would not yield. Can you do that?"

"Oh, aye," the boy breathed, his eyes gone round and full of awe.

"Good lad." Trelayne ruffled his hair, and rose. "Take care, and that goes for all of you."

"Here, now, what's going on?" a stern voice called.

Trelayne grabbed Gerard's shoulder, and pulled him behind the wall of his legs to conceal the sword. "Good Even, captain."

A troop of six guards stood warily on the outskirts of the gathering—they couldn't have been there long, but their faces showed their suspicion. "What are you about, standing in the street like this?" the captain demanded.

"I'm writing a play," Trelayne said, "about the Demon War. These are my actors."

The guards laughed derisively. "This rabble's fit enough for demons," the captain replied, "but who'll be the army?"

"Well it's our first rehearsal," Trelayne protested. "You can't expect much the first night."

"Peasants playing at lies," the captain snorted. "We'll leave you to it."

"Thank you." Trelayne offered a parting bow as the troop moved off, some of the guards still eyeing him suspiciously. "Now where is my sorceress?" he asked, loudly enough to be heard by the retreating soldiers.

Anmoria popped out of her cottage, glancing after the guards with some apprehension. She crossed the street, hopping the ditch, and came to stand beside him. Trelayne stared.

In the six days they had been planning, Anmoria had sewn herself a new dress, an imitation of the high court style, down to the side laces, but all of light woolens, in the dull colors of her people rather than the gleaming silks of the ladies. Full skirts—still shortened in deference to use—gathered at the hip into a tight bodice, cut low to emphasize her breasts, with long draped sleeves which fluttered like wings. Her hands and face were scrubbed, her hair piled up on top of her head to reveal a graceful neck adorned with a simple leather thong and a medallion of the Blue Lady.

Anmoria blushed and looked at her feet. "It is a ball, after all," she stammered, "and I wanted—"she glanced up at him suddenly. "It's not wrong, is it?"

"Oh, no," he murmured, "it looks just right to me."

One of the men whistled, and the others grinned, suddenly smoothing their hair, or adjusting ragged caps.

Trelayne continued staring at her, and Anmoria prompted, "Shouldn't we go? We've a long walk ahead."

"That we should." He offered her his hand. With this couple at its head, the gathering fell into line. The whores and washerwomen partnering with pickpockets and farmers, heads held high, skirts lifted daintily in one hand, as if they'd enough fabric to waste in dragging it on the ground. They did not see many others on the streets they traveled, staying away from the busier places to avoid being spotted until the last moment. Those who did see turned in astonishment to watch the procession, and a few fell in behind to find out where they were going. The road wound upward, so they arrived as the sun was setting, by the great doors of the viceroy's mansion atop the citadel. The doors stood wide for carriages and parties to pass through, with guards dressed more for show than for battle.

Trelayne took a deep breath, and shared a glance with Anmoria. "Away we go," he said, and lead them up to the gate.

Gliding along beside one of the grander carriages, half the group was into the courtyard before the nodding guards cried a halt. Frowning, they stomped to the front of the procession, where Trelayne awaited them.

"What seems to be the trouble?"

The lead man stopped, his mouth working for a moment as he looked from Trelayne to the woman on his arm. "Ah, good evening, sir," the man said, reddening, looking to his fellows for support.

"Good evening," Trelayne replied brightly. "I hope we've not missed the first set. Not that I'm much for dancing any more." He wiggled the crutch, and was rewarded by another uneasy look.

"No, sir, but," the man broke off, fidgeting with his pike.

"Well, then." Trelayne started forward again, placing his crutch and carefully following it.

The guards closed ranks, and a few more came down from the glittering hall to join them.

"It's your company, sir," the man reddened.

"What about them?" Trelayne countered, drawing himself up. Anmoria's steadying grip on his arm clenched a little tighter.

From beyond the guards, a few disembarking lords and ladies turned, and gasped.

"Well, sir, they—"the guard shrugged, gesturing helplessly down the line of ragged people.

Trelayne set his mouth in a hard line. "I was given an invitation, by Viceroy Brisson himself, may the gods give him peace, for myself and my household to attend him ball."

"I don't think this is what he meant, begging your pardon, sir."

"You don't think?" Trelayne shouted. More faces appeared at the doors as handsomely dressed guests came to blink down at the scene. "He meant me to bring my household, the people with whom I break bread, make merry, and bed myself down at night." Anmoria giggled, some of the ladies covered their mouths with delicate kerchiefs.

"These," Trelayne continued grandly, "are they. An unconventional household, but one which suits me well."

Some of the peasants came up around him, while others hovered under the arch, watchful lest a move should be made to close the gate.

"What's the trouble here?" The magistrate, wearing a formal version of his official black robe came down the stairs, then blanched white at the sight of Trelayne.

Trelayne stared back, undaunted.

"He wants to bring all these—"the guard flapped a hand toward Trelayne's retinue—"into the ball, your honor."

"Nonsense," the magistrate snapped. "If he wishes to attend, of course, he is welcome to enter, alone." The queer color of his face gave the lie to these words. His eyes shifted to Trelayne's plain belt, searching for a weapon.

Trelayne said. "These people constitute my household, and I would have them here."

"Sir Trelayne," the magistrate began, his hands upon his hips, "to honor the Code of Chivalry for a—companion—is one thing, but to bring this filth into the viceroy's house is quite another. Send them back, and we shall be honored to have your presence."

Gwenyth pushed her way through the crowd to stand at the magistrate's shoulder, her brows pinched in disapproval, her gaze focused on Anmoria.

Ignoring her, Trelayne said, "Do not force me to defend

that code again. You have insulted my lady, and my people, and I will not stand for it." He shook the end of his crutch.

Some of the nobles laughed, Gwenyth turned several shades of purple, her hands clenched. "Now see here, Trelayne—"

"Shut up, Gwenyth."

"I'll ask you not to treat a lady in this fashion, sir," the magistrate blustered.

"I have just asked the same of you, and you denied me."

"And I'll also ask you to use the proper form of address to an official of the court."

Trelayne spat in the dirt at the magistrate's feet. "You know nothing of honor."

Pulling himself up as if to match Trelayne's height, he snarled, "You seem to have lost yours, young man."

A sound of tramping feet echoed behind them as a large force of guards arrived from their headquarters down below. The peasants muttered amongst themselves, tensing.

"Say that again, you puffed-up little toad, and I'll have you on a spit," Trelayne hissed. The dragonblood scars sprang into searing life, so that he jerked from the force of it, and Anmoria's hand slipped from his arm.

"Guards!" the magistrate bellowed, and the men, still astonished by the insult, lowered their pikes.

"Go!" he cried, sweeping up his crutch and giving the magistrate a hearty crack.

Still bellowing, the man stumbled and knocked Gwenyth to the ground.

The peasants suddenly bristled with weapons, intent

upon flight, prepared to lead the guards a merry chase. Expecting a fight, the guards stood firm, then scattered as their quarry scrambled over or around them, dodging pikes and swords, shrieking with laughter. Anmoria plunged into the chaos, clearing a way for them with the twin daggers her skirt had concealed.

Trelayne balanced, pulled free his crutch, and suddenly, something grabbed his ankle. His damaged leg didn't have the speed to kick it away.

With a jerk, the hand snapped him heavily to the cobbles.

His crutch skittered off across the pavement, overbalancing one guard, causing Anmoria to spin around as it bumped her feet.

"Run!" he screamed.

Five guards filled the gap between them. Anmoria hesitated, her face drained, then snatched up the crutch and ran.

Hands grabbed him, dragging him roughly back toward the house, accompanied by an obscene cackling. "I've got you, bastard," Gwenyth crowed.

A heavy boot kicked him so that he rolled face up. Gwenyth's muddy features confronted him, her teeth bared, more wicked than any demon's.

A reddening kerchief pressed to his head, the magistrate tottered near, and leaned over him. Shaking a tremulous hand, he said, "You'll hang for this, Trelayne. The gallows field will have you yet!"

Distantly, he heard the sounds of combat, his little army fighting for their lives against such odds. Then the sounds cut abruptly off, as the gate swung shut with him on the wrong side. Pulled to his feet, his arms wrenched behind him, Trelayne scanned quickly, praying that Anmoria had won free. To his left, a woman's bare feet kicked beneath the bulk of a guard. Trelayne growled, and tore free from the hands. Then the metal butt of a pike swung down, snapping his head back into oblivion.

# CHAPTER

NINE

### *The Gallows Field*

GROGGILY, TRELAYNE DRAGGED HIMSELF TOWARD the light. Nauseated by the sensation of movement, he waited a moment before actually opening his eyes. His head throbbed, while his knee provided a steady pulse of pain, and the dragonblood scars sizzled on his fingers. The rest of his hands seemed numb, bound with thick rope behind his back. His face pressed against a bristly rug which looked oddly familiar. Squinting at the fibers, he frowned.

"I think he's awake," said a voice not far off.

"Good," a woman replied. "I'd hate for him to miss the big event."

A pointed toe prodded him, and Trelayne rolled, then pushed himself into a sitting position. The surroundings suddenly came into focus, as did the sounds of creaking wheels and snorting horses. He sat on the floor of Gwenyth's carriage, leaning against the soft velvet of one bench. A hulking city guard slouched on the far end, glowering.

Opposite him on the other bench, Gwenyth and the magistrate shared a look. She had clad herself in sturdy hunting garb, while the man wore a shorter robe, revealing sturdy boots. Apparently, they wanted to be ready for anything, but what they feared, Trelayne did not know. He did not even know if the raid had been successful, if he and Derik had once again exchanged lives. He could not see it in their faces, beyond the smug satisfaction that he was in their power.

Inching carefully, keeping his eyes on the guard, Trelayne managed to pull himself up onto the seat. Leaning forward to avoid crushing his bound hands, he gazed from the window. Two rows of mounted guards, bristling with lances and swords, rode alongside—quite a fearsome guard to escort one cripple to his death. Trelayne gave his lop-sided smile.

"I don't see what you've got to smile about, unless you can't wait to feel the rope," Gwenyth said. She did not look directly at him, concentrating instead on the edge of one ragged fingernail her morning toilette must have neglected.

"I am surprised you would consent to ride with such a hardened criminal as myself," he commented absently, returning his eyes to the window.

"Oh," she said, "I wanted to revel in it just a while longer, your descent into madness and filth. Besides, we couldn't fetch a proper executioner's wagon on such short notice."

He grunted in acknowledgment, trying to peer between

the guards, hoping the empty streets could tell him what he dared not ask. The sun's early fire glinted on the helmets and the weapons of the guards.

Exasperated by his inattention, Gwenyth sniped, "I never thought you a good match for myself; I told my parents so when they suggested it."

This barb did not leave him completely untouched: well he recalled the way she had pursued him through the balls and festivals, never missing a chance to display herself for his enjoyment. And he had enjoyed the chase.

He shrugged one shoulder.

The magistrate patted Gwenyth's hand. "You must be proud, my lady, to see your opinion so clearly brought to fruition."

"Oh, pride would seem uncharitable, but I do feel that my insight has been vindicated."

Uncharitable. Trelayne smiled grimly to himself. Let her talk, he would soon be out of earshot.

The carriage lurched around a corner, bumping Trelayne's head against the window frame. He winced, catching a glimpse of the gallows ahead. But what stopped his heart and chilled the fever of his hands was the gallows field. As they creaked up the road, the guards began to pick more carefully, for the field was strewn with corpses. As far as he could see in any direction, bodies lay. The brown garments of peasants mingled with the brightness of the fallen guards' uniforms. Limbs entangled, hair askew, they littered the ground, still shadowed before the coming dawn. Trelayne cursed under his breath, his eyes roving over them, looking for his friends—for the flash of Anmoria's gown, or the floured white of the miller's apron. Even Gerard, innocent little Gerard, sprawled on his face in the dust, as Trelayne once had.

Behind him, Gwenyth forced a laugh.

At the strangled sound, he turned from the ruin of his army, eyes narrowed, fury welling up through the helpless grief.

Beneath the perfect touches of rouge, her face had gone pale. She stared ahead, but could not stop her eyes from flickering to the carnage outside. The magistrate gripped her hand in earnest now, moping his own face with a scented cloth.

"What did you expect? Were you cowering in your house all night, while these people were dying?" Trelayne asked, struggling to keep his voice even. "Did their screams wake you, or did you sleep straight through?"

Gwenyth shut her eyes, her head tilted down as if to shield her ears as well.

"Look at them!" he shouted, and the guard at the end of the bench roused himself to grip his sword more tightly. "This is what war means," Trelayne told her. "You may kill me today, but you will never forget."

The carriage ground to a halt, horses stamping. Trelayne's door popped open and he fell out, grabbed by waiting guards. He craned his neck, searching the dead, as they hauled him to the steps mounting the platform. The guards fell back, joining a small audience of lords and ladies, their fine carriages arrayed behind Gwenyth's own. Gwenyth and the magistrate moved to the front row, their faces twin masks of loathing.

One of the men who lead him carried a rope looped about his arm. The noose opened in a silent cry as he tossed it up, over the gallows arm, and looked to Trelayne.

Trelayne sucked in a deep breath. Sweat beaded on his brow, and his eyes flashed wildly from point to point. Only two men stood by him, but dozens of their companions ringed the platform, all eyes on him. With his crippled leg, with his hands bound, he'd never make it. All that he could hope for was to die by the sword.

Crying out, Trelayne fell against the stout upright at the top step. Head bent, shoulders slumped, he kept his good leg under him.

When the man behind him hesitated, Trelayne slammed a kick into his chest leaving him to tumble back down.

Trelayne yelled like a madman, springing up to the platform, dropping down to roll the other man off his feet.

Somehow, Trelayne rose, trembling, catching the shock and fury on Gwenyth's fair face, the twist of the magistrate's lips as he shouted pointless orders. The guard had righted himself as well, fumbling out his sword.

Trelayne braced himself for the blow. "Have at you!" he cried into the rising sun. Shouts and screams erupted around them, and Trelayne tore his gaze from his attacker's face.

As if on command, the dead rose.

Laborers, whores and children stood from the gallows field, stolen swords clasped in their hands. Many of the guards, too, stood, revealing peasant faces under borrowed helmets. Laughing, Trelayne's army flung itself upon the executioners.

With a snarl of anger and of fear, Trelayne's guard pounced forward, then staggered as the trap burst open beneath him. Two strong hands clasped the edges of the opening, and Derik heaved himself through, with Trelayne's sword clenched in his teeth. Snatching the hilt, Derik whooped with glee as he cut down the guard.

"We live!" Derik bellowed.

"Sweet lady!" Trelayne faltered, barely remaining on his feet.

Derik swung himself behind Trelayne, catching hold of him, and slipping a quick blade through the bonds. Sword tucked beneath his arm, he took a moment to bend over Trelayne's hands, chafing the life back into them. Roger clambered through the opening, followed by the woodcarver and a barkeep.

Trelayne gripped Derik's shoulder. "I've never been so glad to see anyone," he murmured.

Derik snapped, "Save it, we're not out of this yet!"

"At least we're in it together."

At the fierce pride in Trelayne's voice, Derik paused his frantic activity to meet his gaze. "Aye, my lord, we're that." He knelt to the hole and pulled up a long staff—Trelayne's crutch.

Grabbing it, slipping free the hidden sword, Trelayne's trembling hands asked the question he couldn't bear to voice.

"Anmoria said you'd be missing it. Wanted to bring it herself, but I knew you'd not forgive me that." Derik winked, and turned away to the attack.

Ringed about with guards intent on gaining the platform, the defenders cursed and slashed, and more than one city guard fell to a swift blow from the carved crutch. Even from their high ground, Trelayne couldn't tell who had the upper hand. With so many of the peasants clad in guards' livery, both sides succumbed to confusion, striking without killing force, lest the man they struck was one of their own.

Lords and ladies fled in any direction they could, scrambling back into their carriages or trying to catch the horses who reared and thrashed through the battle.

Gwenyth and the magistrate vanished in the fray.

Then, over the wall on the breeze, a bright, clear call of trumpets sounded.

Trelayne strained his eyes, and gasped.

Ranks of knights were at the gate, then through, riding hard. Behind them, a wagon trailed, with trumpeters mounted to either side. At their head as they galloped to the field, the banner of the king waved.

"Hold, I say you!" their leader bellowed. "Hold in the name of the king!"

Stillness rippled across the field.

Guards and peasants lowered their arms, warily stepping back to form a path for the newcomers. In full battle gear, the knights shone beneath the new sun, their horses arrayed in blue and gold, their faces both surprised and grim as they surveyed the conflict around them. As the knights made their way more slowly now down the aisle which opened before them, a figure darted up the path, skirts hoisted above the knee, tousled hair streaming.

"Anmoria!"

She stumbled to a halt on the ground before him, panting, and beaming through her tears. "Oh, love, I feared I'd lost you!"

Unable to answer for the lump which rose in his throat, Trelayne came to the edge of the platform, and dropped down, her strong arms catching and supporting him. With his cheek pressed to hers, Trelayne shut his eyes and shuddered, quiet tears catching in the tangle of her hair.

A smaller party broke from the ranks as the horses halted before the gallows. One of them wore the golden sash and gleaming scroll case of the king's heralds.

From under Gwenyth's carriage, the magistrate crawled, grubby and breathing hard. He offered a hand to Gwenyth, emerging behind him, but she simply glared at it and pulled herself up, shaking off the dirt.

"Sirs," the magistrate began, mopping his face and attempting a smile. "We are indeed pleased to see you." One hand motioned vaguely to the field. "As you can see, we are sorely beset."

The herald nodded once, glancing about him, eyeing Trelayne and his companions, then returned his gaze to the magistrate, the only person of evident authority. "It's well that we arrived when we did, your honor, although this is not the business we came for."

"Business?" he asked blankly, seeming not to know that the men must have been riding for days, long before the battle was dreamed of.

"We are charged to find one Sir Trelayne, of Oak Hollow."

"There he is!" Gwenyth shrilled, pointing. "Arrest him, take him away!"

Frowning, the herald followed her outstretched arm.

By the gallows platform, Trelayne broke away from Anmoria's embrace, leaning heavily on his crutch, glad to have this respite. His leg shook with the effort of supporting him. When his name was spoken, he straightened, sharing raised eyebrows with Derik who jumped down beside him.

The herald swung himself down from his horse, and approached. A few feet short of them, he stopped. Sweeping his short cloak behind him, the herald bent into an elegant bow.

Derik chuckled, while Gwenyth let out something like a growl.

"Firstly," the herald said, "this has been rather slow in coming." He swept his arm toward the wagon which had trundled to a stop not far off. Ready men laid hands upon the vast cloth which had concealed the wagon's contents. "Since you saw fit to leave the army early, sir," he said without rancor, "it took captives and refugees to tell us the tale. Men were dispatched to bring you this."

The cloth fell, and the audience inhaled almost as one. On the bare wood of the wagon rested the skull of the dragon. Blackened by flame, the empty sockets held no malice, though the wicked teeth still clenched as if they longed to tear the flesh of their conqueror. It stood as tall as a man, its terrible jaws half again as long. The brow ridges arched back, creating an impression of perpetual surprise. Whispers flew through the crowd, and many made signs against evil. The nobles drew a little back from the ruined beast of legend. Several of them flushed, looking to Trelayne and quickly away.

Carefully, Trelayne approached his trophy, with Derik and Anmoria beside him. Leaning the crutch against the side of the wagon, sword still in hand, he reached up to touch the bone. Warm beneath his hand, it sent a quiver of power through the dragonblood scars, as if they recognized their own. Grinning, he bent over and kissed its ugly snout. "If they call me a liar again," he murmured under his breath, "I'll cage them in your jaws until they long for mercy." He turned suddenly, scanning the crowd. "Gwenyth! Come here and meet my friends."

A gap opened in the gathering, and he saw Gwenyth, her back turned, skirts taken up to sneak away. She glanced over her shoulder, blanched.

"She said it was a lie," one of the older ladies murmured. "I'm sure she told me so."

Gritting her teeth, and gathering the shreds of her dignity, Gwenyth held herself stiffly, and walked away to be lost among the crowd.

The herald cleared his throat. "My party encountered this one on the road, sir, all of us traveling the same way. But this was not our only purpose." He set his feet, and drew forth a scroll from his case. Unrolling it with care, he held it up before him, the ribbons and seals of the king dangling below.

"Let all to whom these letters come know that His Royal

Majesty, King Agravaine, by blood and blessing, the dread monarch of Corsevale does send warmest greetings to his good and trusted knight, Sir Trelayne of Oak Hollow, son of Marshall, the lord of Drachmare. Having lately been apprised of news that the fair region of Goshan and her capital city are without a viceroy, his Majesty has recalled your brave service during the recent Demon War, and is moved to humbly ask if the said Trelayne, Knight of the Realm and Slayer of the Dragon, would submit himself to serve as Viceroy, the appointment to last throughout his lifetime, with all of the duties and privileges pertaining thereto. Such duties including the maintenance of order and justice, and the supervision—"

At the words "his lifetime", Trelayne swayed, and the crutch dropped to clatter on the ground. Derik caught him, easing him down to sit upon the edge of the wagon. "Have I heard you right?" Trelayne asked.

The Herald glanced up from his reading of those duties and privileges. "Forgive me, Sir, I was not informed of the extent of your injuries. Allow me to be brief."

Numbly, Trelayne nodded.

"His Majesty asks if you would serve as his viceroy in Goshan, and sends his letters and seals affirming your authority should you accept."

Trelayne looked out over the anxious faces of the nobles, and the expectant faces of the peasants. He had not set himself upon such a course, the scope of the responsibility seemed, for a moment, beyond him. Then he spotted movement beyond the knights. A peasant child, his hair flying in joyous abandon, was dancing and chanting his name. A little embarrassed, he ducked his head, his eyes drawn to his stiff right leg, beginning to ache now that the rush of battle was over. Sidelong, he glanced at Derik.

"We were to go adventuring, my friend," Trelayne said softly.

Derik, too, looked up from the damaged knee. He gave a snort of laughter, but his face was serious. "Are there not enough adventures here for you?" He folded his arms, leaning back against the wagon. "Besides, I could do with a bit of a rest. All this rescuing is hard work." He nodded to himself, but let his eyes slip back to Trelayne.

Meeting the surreptitious glance, Trelayne's lop-sided smile grew. He returned his attention to the herald, patiently awaiting him. "I accept."

Cheers and hollers leapt into the air as peasants embraced. The small huddle of nobles seemed to shrink into themselves, but a few mustered feeble applause.

"This man is to be hanged for treason!" the magistrate shouted above the growing din. "I demand justice!"

Studying the apoplectic redness of the magistrate's jowls, the herald inquired, "What is his crime, your honor?"

"Well, he struck me down," the man sputtered, tapping the bruise on his forehead.

"At what provocation?"

Trelayne answered, "This morning, he would have hanged me without trial." With a slight, crooked smile, he continued, "Last night, he held me bound, with neither food nor water; before that, he insulted my lady. That's when I struck him, by the way. All of this after arresting and threatening to execute an innocent man. He furthermore abused the Code of Chivalry by refusing to release his prisoner when the man's life was rightfully won."

"Who was this prisoner, and what was his crime?" the herald asked.

Trelayne presented him. "Derik the wheelwright."

"Derik?" Frowning, the herald reached into his scroll case, bringing out a parchment, and a small bundle. "But I have business with you, as well." He shook out the bundle to reveal a sash of knighthood. "The king wished to reward your valor at Kilsharne's keep, and confer upon you—"

"But he's a peasant!" the magistrate screeched. "The man's a peasant, he doesn't deserve—" he broke off suddenly, his hands freezing as they waved about him.

The herald's eyes had gotten progressively harder, his mouth tighter as he watched. The knights behind him glared down at the one who would dare abuse their Code.

Slender sword in hand, Trelayne leaned forward. He placed the tip of the sword beneath the magistrate's jiggling chin. "You demand justice," he repeated softly. The magistrate trembled, his darting eyes finding no assistance. "Very well, I give you your life. You have one hour to flee those gates. If I hear that you have dared sit in judgment upon another man, so help me I will hunt you down and gut you like the beast you are."

Whimpering, the magistrate took a step back, withdrawing himself from the blade. Then, with a hoarse cry, he ran. Roger the miller blocked the way he had chosen. If

Roger's foot nudged out, or if the mere sight of him set the magistrate into panic, Trelayne couldn't say. But he laughed as loud as any peasant, even as loud as Derik, when the man tumbled, his black robe swirling about him as he fell head over heels to land in the beaten dirt of the gallows field.

If you enjoyed *Winning the Gallows Field*, look for the
second Tale of Bladesend, *Joenna's Ax*

After Joenna's half-orc son is killed in battle, she disguises herself as a man to join the army and avenge him, adding one notch to the handle of her ax for every demons she kills. But when she volunteers to lead a suicide charge of half-orc scouts, she risks her secret and her own mission to try to save them. Rewarded for her prowess with a grant of land and ownership of her half-orc man-at-arms, Joenna plots to rescue all of the half-orcs from the king's plan to destroy these reviled bastards—making herself a traitor along with them. When their haven is discovered, Joenna leads the half-orcs in a desparate fight against a famous warrior and his knights in the hopes of winning their freedom and claiming their humanity.

Elaine Isaak, writing as E. C. Ambrose, is also the author of The Dark Apostle series, from DAW books : magic, intrigue, medieval surgery

*Elisha Barber, July, 2013*
England in the fourteenth century: a land of poverty and opulence, prayer and plague, witchcraft and necromancy. Where the medieval barber-surgeon Elisha seeks redemption as a medic on the front lines of an unjust war, and is drawn into the perilous world of sorcery by a beautiful young witch.

In the crucible of combat, at the mercy of his capricious superiors, Elisha must attempt to unravel conspiracies both magical and mundane, as well as come to terms with his own disturbing new abilities. But the only things more dangerous than the questions he's asking are the answers he may reveal...

Traditional Fantasy novels by the same author:

*The Singer's Crown*
Available in a variety of e-book formats from Rocinante

When his uncle murders his family to take the throne, Prince Kattanan DuRhys is the only royal left alive. . . at a terrible cost. Stripped of his manhood, Kattanan travels as a court singer from one wealthy patron to the next. Given as a courtship gift to the young Princess Melisande, Kattanan feels the stirring of emotions he thought were denied him. But her jealous fiancée has other plans--and the sinister magic to carry them out.

Must Kattanan sacrifice his song to win his kingdom, and the woman he loves?

*The Eunuch's Heir*
Available in a variety of e-book formats, from Rocinante

Prince Wolfram of Lochalyn can't possibly live up to the reputation of his father, the Blessed Rhys, so why bother to try? Until a series of self-started catastrophes plunges him into the midst of the growing refugee population. They claim to be fleeing a war, and only Wolfram sees the danger that lurks in their mysterious ways. But his love for an exotic stranger, and his concern for the princess who pursues him collide with a more terrible struggle, in which his kingdom may fall and his very Goddess be brought to Her knees. Discredited by his past and disdained by his own mother, Wolfram must find the truth of his birth, and fight to make amends for all that he's done—or be seduced by the darkness of distant power.

### The Bastard Queen
Available in a variety of e-book formats, from Rocinante

Beloved bastard of an unloved king, Fiona will do almost anything to please her father, even studying magic though she never shows more than a spark of talent. But the plague that grips their city sends her to work with the dying, as enmity builds between the two peoples her father has brought together. When arson burns a hospital, everyone blames the growing racial tension, until an unexpected suspect comes from the woods on a spirit-quest destined to uncover the secrets of Fiona's past. Then Reynaud, long Fiona's suitor, suddenly asks to marry her sister. Struggling to find a cure for the plague, Fiona becomes ever more convinced that its emergence is no coincidence—and that Reynaud may be leading a conspiracy that will end in genocide.

# About the Author

Elaine Isaak is the author of *The Singer's Crown* (Eos, 2005), and its sequels, as well as the "Tales of Bladesend" epic novellas comprising *Joenna's Ax* in full-length, and *Winning the Gallows Field*. As E. C. Ambrose, she writes "The Dark Apostle" historical fantasy novels about medieval surgery, which began with *Elisha Barber* (DAW 2013), and continue with *Elisha Magus* (2014), *Elisha Rex* (2015), *Elisha Mancer* (2017), and concluding with *Elisha Daemon* (2018). Her short fiction has won the Tenebris Press Flash Fiction contest and appeared in the New Hampshire Pulp Fiction series, *Fireside* magazine and *Uncle John's Bathroom Reader*. A graduate of the Odyssey Speculative Fiction workshop, she has returned to teach there as well. In addition to writing and teaching about writing, Elaine works part time as an adventure guide and rock climbing instructor. Visit www.TheDarkApostle.com or www.ElaineIsaak.com to find out why you do not want to be her hero.

facebook.com/ElaineIsaak
or twitter @elaineisaak